The Haunting of Anna-Rose

Erica J Whelton

Publisher: Sunseri Design Publishing
ISBN: 978-1-956069-17-4

Printed in the United States of America

To my beautiful U.S. Navy friends! You are all so dear to me. Thank you for all the wonderful years of friendship.

Books by this Author:

Medium with a Heart—Paranormal Cozy Series:
Premedicated Murder (book 1)
Replicated Murder (book 2)
Organized Murder (book 3)
Inherited Murder (book 4)
Crafted Murder (book 5)

Finding Herself—Women's Fiction Series:
Mandy's Story: Courage (book 1)
Becca's Story: Purpose (book 2)
Caroline's Story: Serenity (book 3)

Women's Fiction
Decoding Us (Coming July 2023)

Chapter One: Anna-Rose (1882)

My excitement bubbled up as the train rumbled into the station. The weeks of endless travel would soon be over, and I would start my life with my new husband, James Collins.

We met at a social several months ago back home in Virginia, and it was love at first sight. From the moment our eyes met, we were inseparable.

However, James was planning to head to Texas to start a homestead and begged me to join him. Thrilled at the idea of adventure in the West, I agreed.

The plan was for us to marry and then he would leave for Texas, get everything set up before I joined him a few months later.

He had already purchased the 600-acre property with a small farmhouse on it. The former owner had passed on, leaving no heirs or anyone to take it over. It was owned by the bank. James bought it sight unseen from an advertisement in the paper.

"Imagine it, Anna-Rose," he'd said. "Rolling hills, field after field of cotton, oats, corn. It will be beautiful."

"I can picture it."

"I'll work the fields."

"And I'll have your meals ready when you come in from working."

"That will be wonderful. We'll be the perfect family."

We made big plans, and I couldn't wait to start our life together. However, my family did not react as I'd expected. I fully believed they would be happy with me finally wanting to marry.

"Anna-Rose, you barely know this man. We know nothing about him." My father roared.

"But I know him. I love him."

"How is he going to support you?"

"He's a farmer and we'll raise crops and cattle."

"That's not a living, Anna-Rose. A banker, like me, that's a living."

My mother's reaction was to spend the next three days in bed suffering from a headache. It was of little concern to me. I was nearly twenty, and more than ready for a husband and starting my own household. Many of my girlfriends had already married. I was one of the last and practically a spinster.

But once mother had recovered, she sat me down to discuss running a household. Actually, it was to lecture me on my lack of skills. This was mostly her fault for keeping me away from much of this type of work. She managed the household duties.

"You do not know how to cook. You don't clean. How will you do those things?" She started.

"I know how to do those things." I simply didn't need to.

"You need to learn. You cannot keep a man happy, especially out in the wild like that, without knowing those things."

She then listed all the things I needed to learn; cooking with few supplies, how to make soap, candles making, laundry.

"And what do you know of caring for an ill person? There probably won't be a doctor. You'll need to know about taking care of injuries, illnesses."

"I have plenty of time to learn."

I immediately started asking friends, neighbors, anyone in town I could think that I could learn from. Then I found a book called *Housekeeping in Old Virginia Containing Contributions from 250 of Virginia's Noted stay-at-home parent Distinguished for Their Skill in the Culinary Art and Other Branches of Domestic Economy.*

It had the most useful information. There was a list of everything, from food to medicine to cleaning. It was a collaboration of many, many housewives that were having to survive after the war.

"This is what I needed." I hugged it to my body and then studied each page and recipe until I had them memorized. I would also try to practice as much as I could before I left to join him.

With only a few days before he would leave for Texas, we married in a simple ceremony that my mother cried through. I had made my dress from one of my traveling gowns with an added train and additional lace. He had on a new suit.

"This is the first new suit I've owned since I was a lad." He confessed once the ceremony was over. "It has been mostly hand-me-downs from my older brother."

"It looks dapper on you." I put my hand on his arm with a giggle and a flutter in my stomach as I thought about what would come soon, the wedding night.

I had already gotten a talk from my mother about *wifely duties* in the bedroom. It had not been helpful and only added to my anxiety.

"You must submit to your husband. It is the proper thing to do. If you do your job, he will treat you well by providing and protecting you."

I got a different tale from one of my newly married girlfriends.

"You know us girls are told to just submit." She whispered. "My mother said to close my eyes until it was over. Just between us, I enjoy it."

"Maribeth! That is scandalous." I giggled.

"You'll see!" She giggled and slapped playfully at my arm.

Secretly, I hoped things with James would go like this. We got on so well outside of the bedroom. I wanted that fairytale to continue into the bedroom. I didn't want to be one of those ladies who simply submitted, but more carefree, like some of my girlfriends seemed.

Unfortunately, it was not enjoyable at all. He was rough to the point of almost cruel, or perhaps that's how it was supposed to go. Either way, I didn't enjoy it.

I followed Maribeth's mother's words by keeping my eyes closed, praying until it was over. After he fell asleep, I wept quietly. Had I disappointed him or were my expectations too high?

Being my first time, I brushed it off as inexperience. It would get better because I loved him and outside of the bedroom, he was a gentleman. The perfect man for me, and the one I couldn't wait to start my life with.

He left a few days later, and then my months of waiting started. I used that time to prepare recipes, gather supplies I would need, and learn all I could.

When I finally started packing, I had to be selective with my dresses. Most of my clothing would not be suitable for a pioneer, homesteading life. I bought bolts of linen and wool and made shirtwaists and long skirts without the bustles and trim that my current gowns had.

"I'm sure I won't need the corsets, at least not these."

"You must wear a corset, Anna-Rose. It is the proper way to dress." Mother scowled at me.

"Mother, it won't be practical. I will be milking cows, butchering chickens, and farming." I laughed.

She was the one who had already warned me about life in the West. I had been honing my skills the best I could, and knew that a corset would not be practical, at least not these.

These were for going into the city, having garden parties or dinner parties. Not doing hard labor.

"Oh, Anna-Rose, that's not how we raised you." She melted into tears and left me to pack alone.

The entire train ride, I could barely sit still. I stared out at the passing scenery, enjoying the changing landscape with each passing mile, and rereading his letters about what our new house was like. With each word he wrote, I tried to imagine what my new home would look like and the life we would soon build together.

It all felt like a fairy tale come to life.

Maribeth had given me a stack of journals and a new pen with an inkwell. Even with the rock of the train, I captured some of what I saw on my trip. My thoughts, fears, and hopes. One day, I will share these journals with my children.

As I stepped off the train into the Texas heat, I looked for James in the crowd. I was eager to start our life together.

"Anna-Rose!" I heard his voice call out.

"James." I waved. Relief flooded my body.

"Oh, I missed you, my love." He pulled me into his arms.

"I missed you as well." I touched his face. "You grew a beard."

"I did. It's a different country out here." I'd missed his deep chuckle. "Let's get your trunks and get you home."

We gathered my things and put them in his wagon.

We rode from the station through town. The rutted road rocked the wagon, and I held on to James and the side, so I didn't topple off. I giggled with glee. I had waited months to be here in this moment with my handsome husband.

The streets back home were brick or cobblestone, so it wasn't quite this uneven, though the cobblestones could be bumpy.

The store fronts here were wooden and much smaller than those back home too. It was quaint.

"We have more than a day's drive back to Wisteria." James said. "I brought supplies so we can stop tonight."

As I looked at the sights, I simply nodded. I knew with the train station being closer to Fort Worth, it would take us time to get to our new home. But I didn't mind, it was all so exciting.

I'd never left my hometown of Richmond, Virginia. This was a new adventure in so many ways. New husband, new state, and a long train ride followed by this day and a half wagon ride.

As it got dark, we pulled to the side, finding a flat spot to make camp for the night. He got busy building a fire while I made a bed under the wagon. Then I found the food he had brought along and put together a meal for us.

It wasn't much. A few eggs and bacon, along with some corn cakes and fried potatoes. This was an easy meal. I had gotten good at more complex recipes. I couldn't wait to show off my skills.

"This is wonderful." He gushed as he ate it up.

I simply smiled. After the two weeks of travel and the excitement, I was too tired to eat, only nibbling at my food.

When we finished our meal, I cleaned up our dishes and packed them back away. Then we laid on the blankets and stared at the stars. He told me all about our homestead and how wonderful it was.

"It will be perfect once you are there." He wrapped his arms around me, kissing my neck.

"James, we can't... do that here." I giggled.

"Oh, Anna-Rose, don't be prude. We are married. This is perfectly fine."

"But what if someone sees?" I snuggled into him.

"Nobody is around. Come here."

It was not nearly as enjoyable as it should have been, but it wasn't as awful as the first few times. I fell asleep wrapped in his arms with a smile on my face.

The next day, after I made another quick meal, we started toward home as the sun came up.

I had been exhausted yesterday, so it gave me plenty of time to get reconnected. I told him all about my travels. It had been a few weeks' worth of travel because there was not a direct route from Virginia to Texas yet. The railroads were growing daily, and a more direct route was nearly complete, but I had to stop in St. Louis first, and then catch a different train to get here.

"I thought I'd never arrive. It felt endless."

"Well, the important part is you're here now. We can begin our life together." He patted my leg.

His touch startled me. For some reason, it caught me off guard. I wasn't yet used to him touching me casually like a married couple, even if I had touched him when I first saw him. I would have to get comfortable with him.

He laughed, "Anna-Rose, why so jumpy?"

"I'm sorry. I'm just tired from the trip."

"We'll get home, and you can rest."

He once again told me all about the house. He had only just completed the repair work and added additional rooms for us, our family we hoped to have.

"Had you seen it when I arrived, you would not believe how much it's change."

"You said it was one-room."

"It was. Now it has all the space we need."

He had asked me to order furniture to be shipped. I had so much fun looking through the catalogs, picturing each item in my new home.

"The furniture should arrive in two weeks, and then our home will be complete." I informed him.

"It will be complete the moment you step in it." He grinned.

I blushed at his kind words and handsome smile that was meant for only me.

We arrived in Wisteria a few hours later.

It resembled the other small towns we had passed through. Rutted dirt roads and wood structures, but this was our home now and it felt different. People waved or smiled as we passed. A few men called out to James. I beamed with pride from my perch next to him.

"You're happy?" He asked.

"Yes, so happy."

Then, as we rounded the last mile to our home, I took in the tall pine trees and oaks. So similar to Virginia, yet so wild and untamed.

The house came into sight. A one-story clapboard farmhouse with a wide porch wrapped all around. He'd painted it a pale yellow with dark green shutters, just as I'd asked him to do. It was perfect.

I gasped at the sight. "Oh, James..."

"Do you like it, my love?"

"So very much. Thank you for making this for us."

"Welcome home, darling." He kissed me lightly before whisking me into the house and into my new role as wife.

Chapter Two: Lindsey (January Present Day)

I stood with my box of personal items, taking one last look around my office space. For 10 years, I sat at this desk. I couldn't believe this was happening. Happy New Year to me.

The security guard cleared his throat.

"I'm sorry. I'm going." *Geez, give a girl a minute to mourn.*

Heaving a sigh, I did the walk of shame to my car, loaded my measly box into the trunk and sat trying to process the last hour of my life.

I was laid off with no warning, no true idea of why.

Well, that's not entirely true. They needed a scapegoat, and that was me. The new Vice President had taken one look at me and instantly didn't like me. The feeling was mutual, and it had been an uphill battle ever since.

It had been five months of treading through this toxic environment, trying not to upset the balance, but that was over now.

They were struggling to stay in business and all I could think was using me as a fall guy, so to speak. Trying to blame me for the loss caused by the Vice President.

She lost the client account, not me. She didn't even know our business or understand the relationship with our client the way I did. I had worked with them for years and after only one conversation with her; they dropped us.

Unfortunately, I couldn't prove she was the reason. The client simply said they had found a new accountant. This turned into a case of he said, she said, or in this case, she said, she said with me being on the losing end.

I put the car in gear and headed home, trying to get my mind off of how I was going to tell Derek. I turned the radio volume up as loud as I could stand trying to hum along, but it wasn't enough to distract me.

"What am I going to say to him? What is he going to think?" I sobbed out.

Sure, we had money saved, and they gave me a severance, as they were calling it a layoff, not firing. This was likely done to appease me, so I wouldn't sue. I don't know if I could, but they made it clear this was not a firing.

In all honesty, it wasn't worth the fight. They'd be out of business in a year or less, and I'd find another job before then.

If I thought of it that way, it was almost a blessing to get out before the shit really hit the fan.

"Ahhh... This sucks!" I screamed at the windshield as I squeezed the life out of the steering wheel.

Then looked around embarrassed, hoping nobody in the adjacent cars thought I was having a case of road rage.

As quickly as I had that thought, I was back to banging on the steering wheel and ugly crying in frustration, not caring who witnessed.

As I rounded the corner to our street, our two story contemporary house came into view. I gasped when I noticed that Derek's car was in the driveway.

When I pulled in next to it, I noticed there were boxes stacked in the back seat.

"What in the world?" I stepped out and headed into the house through the open front door. I looked at it as if it was a foreign object. Why was it open? "Derek? Are you here?"

As I turned into the house, I nearly tripped over a duffel bag and another box that was near the front door. What was going on?

"Oh, Lindsey, um, I'm... what are you doing home?"

"I got fired today... well, laid off."

My throat tightened as I spoke the words. Saying it made it really.

I stepped towards him, hoping for his arms as comfort. Instead, he took a step back. That's when my brain clicked in.

"What's going on? Are you... going somewhere?"

"I think... well, we need to talk." He looked at his feet and then looked at me again, tears in his eyes.

"What's wrong? Is it your mom? Is she okay?" His mom had stage 4 breast cancer and hadn't been doing well with the treatments.

"No, not her. She's okay at the moment. It's us. I... I have met someone and I'm filing for divorce."

"Wait? What? Divorce... You *met* someone else." I felt lightheaded, and I reached a hand towards the nearby wall to steady myself. The cold marble tile wall grounded me in the moment. Today was not my day. "I don't understand."

"Yes, I met someone else, and I'm in love with her." He picked up the duffel bag, putting the strap over his shoulder. "I'm moving in with her and have already talked with a lawyer. He'll be sending you the paperwork soon. We can discuss dividing assets later, but for now, I'm leaving."

"No, wait, you can't just leave right now. I mean, *seriously*, were you just going to leave? Let me come home to find you were gone... and then what?" A cloud of red fogged my vision as my emotions switched from hurt to anger. "I was *just* going to figure it out and be *okay* with this? Well, I'm not okay! This is completely out of left field. We were happy. What happened?"

Angry tears were forming in my eyes. I wiped at them violently. I would not give him the satisfaction of my tears. Not until I had answers.

"*You* were happy. I haven't been happy for a while, but you were too self-absorbed to notice. Worrying more about having a baby, not on us."

"You wanted a baby, too. It wasn't just for me."

"At first, yes, but then you became... I don't know... obsessed with it, like it was a job. A very stressful job. I can't and won't go through this anymore." He looked at me with a stony expression. "Now I'm leaving, and my lawyer will contact you soon with the divorce papers."

He dropped his house key on the front table, grabbed the box that was sitting there, adjusted the duffel bag's strap, then walked out the door. He didn't look back.

Without a free hand to shut the front door, he simply walked out, leaving it open. I just stared at the door with all the anger and hurt, willing it to shut on its own. I could hear him loading the car, turning it on, and then the hum of the engine as he drove away. Out of my life.

Good riddance to bad rubbish. As my grandmother used to say.

I stood there for probably just seconds, but it felt like a lifetime. My body was numb from the shock, but finally, my brain and heart communicated with each other, and I collapsed into a puddle on the floor. Tears pouring from eyes.

I crawled to the door and shut it so I could fall apart properly and privately. What had happened to my life in just a few brief hours?

Jobless and alone.

~ ~

The next day, after a fitful night, I stumbled to the kitchen for coffee and then pulled up lawyers on my computer. I had to find one, so I didn't get further screwed in this deal. How could he just leave like that?

If I were honest with myself, I could see he had pulled away a bit lately, working late, being on his computer into the night. We still slept in the same bed, had sex regularly, but as he said, it was more of a scheduled thing because of trying for a baby.

But to just fall in love with someone else without warning, no signs. It wasn't like we'd been fighting. Though, outside of the sex, we rarely talked anymore.

I cursed as I thought it all out. He was right, and I knew it.

Yesterday had kicked me down. It took my job and my husband from me, but today I was going to make a plan and take my life back. Starting with ensuring I was protected from whatever he and his lawyer had put in the divorce papers.

I didn't know which lawyer Derek had hired, but he had said he, so I figured finding a woman would ensure I didn't accidentally pick the same one. After making an appointment with one, I moved on to creating a new bank account.

That's when I realized he had already taken money out of our joint account. It looked like it was "his share" which meant I had to act fast before he got greedy and decided that wasn't enough.

I opened my own online account and then withdrew almost all the money from the joint account, leaving just enough to keep the account open, but barely. This was my share, and I would not let him take it.

I noticed that I'd been paid my last paycheck, but not the severance. I didn't want him to get that. It was a lot of money.

I called up my old company to see if it had been processed yet. Meagan was my friend, or at least had been, so I hoped she would do this for me.

"Hello, Meagan Taylor here."

"Hey, Meag, it's Lindsey."

"Oh, um, hey. How're you doing?" Her voice cracked.

"I'm okay." I hesitated to say too much, as I wasn't yet sure who could be trusted there. "I was calling to see if my severance check had been cut yet?"

"Not yet. It is in the approval stages now. What's up?"

"I have new banking information, long story, but I was hoping I could update it." *Please, oh please, let this work. Something had to, right?*

"Absolutely. I can do that for you right now."

"Oh, thank you!" I read off the information, then she repeated it back. "Oh.my.gosh, you are a lifesaver. I really appreciate this."

"Of course." She lowered her voice. "I'm glad you caught me. I'm going to be giving notice soon. This place is about to implode."

"I know. The writing is on the wall."

"Well, keep in touch, please?" She said, a little too cheerily.

"Of course. You too."

We hung up. I had no intentions of keeping in touch, but really hoped that the severance would come through before the company fell apart.

With that taken care of, I needed to figure out a job. I didn't know if I could go back to account management. My spirit was crushed, and I hated the work.

Unfortunately, it was all I had done in my adult career.

As I browsed through the different online job sites, the realization hit me. I didn't want to work for someone in a cube where they could lie and treat you crappy until one day, with little to no warning, they just let you go. I felt a lump in my throat, and I could feel the tears forming.

A random ad popped on the side of the screen. It caught my eye. A bed-and-breakfast but at a farm. They called it agritourism. Interesting.

I clicked.

It was a small working farm that you could stay at and help around the farm. They had various crops and animals. Depending on what was in season would dictate the chores that needed to be done.

A light bulb moment.

"I could do this."

I had some experience working on a farm. From the time I was eight until I was fifteen, I spent summers with my aunt and uncle on their farm in southern Virginia, close to the North Carolina state line.

From fifteen until I met and married Derek, I had helped my dad flipping homes. I had done it all, except electrical. That was my brother Bryan's specialty. But I could do everything from laying tile to hanging drywall to painting, and everything in between. I had done fencing and some roofing, though I didn't like heights of being on a roof.

There was a lot of work to be done on a farm. I knew it wasn't just animals or growing crops. So, if I decided on doing this farming thing, I could do most everything myself.

I started searching for other farms to get an idea of activities and cost. I read reviews and travel blogs. This was a thing. A real thing. I was getting jazzed.

"This could be my fresh start."

The only problem was getting out of this city and getting to the country.

"Where to go? Where to go?" I drummed my fingers on the table as I thought.

I lived in California, which was an excellent place for farming. But the land here was expensive, and I didn't have enough saved to afford it.

Plus, I wanted as much distance as I could from Derek. A few states between us would be nice.

I did random searches for property. Starting in Arizona and Nevada, then going out from there. When I got to Texas, something about it spoke to me. It helped that the land was reasonably priced, at least compared to some of the other places I had looked.

The state was huge, with so many options for places to live. I had to narrow it down to a region and then find a city.

I searched and researched until I found it.

Wisteria.

That sounds beautiful. Close to Waco, a few hours to Dallas, Houston, or Austin. I could grow a variety of vegetables and fruit. Maybe I could get a small herd of goats, a flock of chickens, and maybe a dog.

For years, I'd wanted a dog, but Derek didn't like them, said he was allergic, and they made him nervous. Even more reason to get one to keep him away.

"Derek." I growled under my breath.

I looked for properties. A fraction of the cost of anything in this area. I flipped through several before one spoke to me. Everything about it was familiar. Goosebumps raised on my arms as I scrolled through the pictures.

"Oh, wow... This is awesome."

I smiled as I scrolled through each picture. The sense of familiarity got stronger and stronger with each one. It was almost as if I knew this house.

"That just means it's meant to be." I giggled.

It would take a bit of work as it looked like it hadn't been lived in for some time. My construction experience would come in handy.

With my severance and savings, I had more than enough to put a down payment on it. Then, once Derek and I sold this house, as part of the divorce, I would have money to live on for a bit. This house could easily sell for more than we owed and once we split it, I would be all set.

My chest tightened a little at the thought of leaving my home. I looked around at the familiar walls, furnishings, windows. This had been our home for five or six years now.

It had been our dream house, or so I thought. We were going to raise a family here. That hadn't happened after several years of trying. Miscarriages and infertility combined.

Before I chickened out, I clicked on the link to contact the agent on the listing.

I squealed.

"Oh my gosh, this is happening!" Or at least I was taking steps forward.

Chapter Three: Lindsey (March Present Day)

"Lindsey, you know this is insane, right?" My best friend, Simone, chastised me.

"No, it's the right amount of sane."

"How?" She stood with a half-taped box in her hand. "How is moving clear across the country from me sane?"

"It's not clear across the country. A day's drive or two if you break it up."

"Not a day's drive. It's almost exactly 23 hours from here to there." She picked up her phone to show me the map. "To me, a day is daylight hours. This... *This* right here is insanity." She leaned over and hugged me. "I'm just going to miss you like crazy."

"You can come with me?"

"Now you *are* talking crazy. I wouldn't move there for anything in the world. Not even you, my dear friend." She got back to packing. "But you know, I'm not surprised that of all my friends, you are the one doing this?"

"Wait? What's that mean?"

"You're an old soul. Always have been. You seem to be drawn to simpler things. You pick retro styles more often than more modern things. I mean, take this house. This was more about Derek than you."

I looked around. It was a contemporary style with clean lines, broad, tall windows, and an open concept. I preferred something with some history and cozy spaces, like the house in Texas. Maybe she was right.

"You're thinking about it now, aren't you?" She laughed.

"No." I chuckled. "Yeah, I'd never thought of it that way. Remember when I was looking at those ranch houses near Lemon Grove? Derek hated them, but I was in love. I could have really pictured myself there."

"Those were definitely more you."

Her words took some of the sting out of having to leave this house. I had always thought of this as our dream house, but it may have been more about settling and trying to force a relationship that just wasn't meant to be.

After working side-by-side for an hour or two, we called it quits so we could meet our other friends for dinner. We cleaned up and then headed over to the restaurant.

We chatted quietly in the back of the Uber as we planned to have many drinks tonight. Since I would head out to Texas in just a few short days, this was my farewell party.

"Hey, girl!" Rachel called out from the bar. She handed me a margarita before I could even reply to her greeting.

"Well, thank you." I leaned forward to hug her and then greeted Bailey.

"I can't believe you are leaving us," Bailey said as our quick hug ended. "Things won't be the same without you here."

"I'll tell you what I told Simone. You're welcome to join me on my journey."

There was a collective no. They all had lives here, and I didn't expect them to say yes. But for me, there was nothing else here, well, except for my three wonderful friends.

We toasted my path to self-discovery and new opportunities.

"You all agree with me though that she is insane, right?"

"I don't know." Rachel shrugged. "I get it. The old soul thing and all."

"You were always my favorite." I threw my arm around her and then signaled the server for another round. "Simone said pretty much the same about the old soul part. My mom's being telling me that my whole life."

"Yeah, you just have this light about you that says you've done life before."

"Or the way you think about things, um, just differently. Wiser, more thoughtfully." Bailey added.

"Plus, I think leaving everything behind is incredibly brave. Starting a new venture. It sounds exciting!" Rachel smiled.

"I'm actually a bit jealous." Bailey admitted.

"What? Jealous. You have a wonderful husband, a family. All you need is the white picket fence and the dog, and you will have the American dream. Well, at least for some." I laughed.

"I do have a wonderful husband." She looked down at her new wedding ring.

They had recently renewed their vows, and he gave her a gorgeous new diamond ring with their birthstones and their children's birthstone on the band.

Rachel was married with children, too. It was just Simone and me as the single ladies of the group. Though for a minute, I had been married.

"See? And I don't have that. Plus, Derek is here and that new woman of his is, too. What if I run into them? Worse, what if they have children? It would just be a constant reminder of what I couldn't have, what I lost."

A lump formed, and my eyes burned. I grabbed the freshly made margarita and took a big gulp before the tears started in earnest.

Simone squeezed my hand. She had been with me through all the miscarriages and infertility.

"Let's not think of the bad. You're on to bigger and better things!" She raised her glass as a toast. "To your new life!"

"To your new life!" The other two said, raising their glasses.

We clinked the glasses together with a laugh.

"Alright, should we order food? I'm starving." Bailey asked, grabbing her menu.

"And another round of drinks!" Rachel spun around, looking for our server. Her text chimed. "Grr, why can't they handle things while I'm out?"

She was always getting messages from her family while we were out. This was going to go on off and on all night.

"They can't find Hazel's blanket." She muttered as she typed out her response.

By the end of the night, I was not seeing straight and had forgotten all my troubles. We took an Uber back to my house for a sleepover. It was the last night in my house, and I didn't want to be alone.

Tomorrow, the movers would come take my things and they would start driving them to Texas. I'd stay a few more days in a hotel until all the final paperwork for the house and we had our first mediation to split assets.

It's amazing how fast things can happen when all the parties involved just want it over with.

As the girls and I settled on sleeping bags in my living room, I looked around at them. I would definitely miss this and them. I didn't yet know anyone in Wisteria.

Though I had been talking with the real estate agent, Linda, almost daily for the past couple of months. She seemed like a sweetheart of a lady, and I couldn't wait to meet her in person.

I had big plans for my tiny farm. I wanted to plant a garden and raise animals. There were some metro areas not too far from me and I hoped it would mean I could offer schools or day cares to come learn at the farm.

Maybe I could get a small trailer and travel around as a petting zoo of sorts.

It just felt like I had so many choices. My dreams were probably bigger than the reality of what I could pull off, but without those dreams, I had nothing.

During my daydreaming, I drifted off to sleep. The light from the windows came streaming in, waking us up.

My friends and I were solemn as we packed up the last of my things. One by one, they said goodbye through tears and hugs and promises of staying in touch.

Simone was the last to leave.

"I can't let you go." She said as we hugged. "If I let go, that will mean you're really leaving."

"I know." Tears formed in my eyes at the thought. "I hope you'll at least come visit."

"You know I will as soon as I'm able."

She wiped a tear from my face, making us both laugh, then she turned and walked out. I watched her go.

Once she was gone, I grabbed my overnight bag that held more than a few nights' worth of stuff and loaded it into my car. Checking the clock, I had time to grab a quick coffee.

I drove to my favorite local spot.

"Hey, Lindsey!" The barista, Sam, said. "The usual, to-go?"

"You know me so well, Sam." I smiled, giving a big tip.

I didn't mention to him that this was likely my last time to come here. No point in more goodbyes. I would soon just become that customer that doesn't come in any longer.

I got home with just minutes to spare before the movers were due.

When they arrived, they made quick work of my few items. I had sold quite a lot and gave some to Derek. I kept only enough to get me started. Plus, I could buy new things in Texas once I got there.

Linda had said there were some antique pieces in the house. I'd seen them in pictures, but until I could touch them, I wasn't sure what I would save.

After the movers left, I walked from room to room, taking in the emptiness, feeling the loss, and then the relief of moving on. I had choices now. I had new opportunities.

Derek had been right. We hadn't been happy, not for a long time. I just was so stuck in my rut that I hadn't realized it.

It took a big shake up for me to get unstuck. I was ready for my new adventure in my new home.

Chapter Four: Lindsey (April Present Day)

It had been a little over three months since I sent that first fateful email and set my life on a much different path. I was now on the last few miles of my journey to my new home. With each passing mile, my excitement grew. I couldn't wait to start this journey.

Derek and I had sold our house easily. We split the profit 60/40. My lawyer had been good. Damn good. She had argued with facts and precedents, stating that he had wrongfully terminated our marriage agreement. She made it sound like a business deal.

Listening to her had me squirming in my seat. I'd never thought of my marriage in that way, but it got me what I needed to start over.

His lawyer seemed to be out of his element, and in his frantic state, advised Derek to take that deal rather than fight it, saying a judge would look at his abandonment negatively. I think he was an idiot to give up so quickly, but I would not point out something that was in my favor.

My lawyer, on the other hand, was a shark in a pinstriped pencil skirt suit and stiletto heels. She ate guys like Derek for lunch and got their ex-wives everything and anything they wanted and deserved. All I wanted was enough money to start over in a new state and start my agritourism business.

The divorce wouldn't be official for a few months. We had to wait six months from the filing date for it to be granted, but we had to split assets earlier as we had both moved on from the house. That had been done in mediation.

I took my money and ran to Wisteria, Texas. Small-town of roughly 6,000. Two stop lights and a grocery store that was actually labeled as General Store. How cute is that?

I drove through and then south of town where my property sat. It was a rough ride over the overgrown driveway, but as I pulled up at the house, I had a dizzying déjà vu moment. Goosebumps rose on my skin and the hair on the back of my neck pricked.

I wrote it off as excitement and maybe exhaustion. I had been driving for what felt like days. Simone was right about that drive being long. It took me two full days and a night in a hotel just outside of El Paso.

I parked in front of the house, just feet from where the real estate agent was standing. She waved, pushing off of the car as she came to greet me. She was a middle-aged woman in a pale pink blouse and light gray dress pants, and almost exactly how I'd pictured her.

The house was an old clapboard farmhouse with faded green paint with hints of yellow peeking through in spots. There were a few broken windows and a gorgeous wrap-around porch. It was a T shaped house with one-story on one side, then two stories on the other. The roof was missing shingles and more than likely leaked like a sieve. I started a mental list of what would need to be done first.

New roof. Check.

Fresh paint. Check.

"Hi, Lindsey, right?"

"Yes, hi."

"It's nice to finally meet in person." She said as she rushed over to hug me.

"Yeah, nice to put a face to the voice. Thanks for meeting me here, Linda. It's even more beautiful in person." I scanned the overgrown yard. It needed a lot of work, but in my eyes, it was perfect.

I could picture a couple of picnic tables clustered under that sprawling oak tree. I'd add a chicken coop over there, looking at a flat spot where it appeared to have had some structure.

"Umm, yeah," she gave it a once-overlook. "It's something all right. Needs a lot of T.L.C." She looked from the house to me. "As I told you, it hasn't been lived in for years."

I nodded and looked around again. There was so much to do. I was thankful that my dad and brother offered to come help. They will be here at the end of the week.

That gave me time to assess and gather supplies.

"Well, let me show you the inside." She walked up the few steps to the front door. I followed.

The boards creaked and cracked a little. I hope they will hold.

New porch and steps. Check.

She inserted the key; it resisted at first due to age and rust, but she wiggled it until the lock gave and the door swung wide. The eerie déjà vu feeling came back, causing a bit of an overwhelming vertigo. I swayed on my feet, but quickly regained my composure.

"Are you okay?" Linda looked concerned.

"Yeah, I'm sorry. I think I'm just tired from the drive. San Diego is a long way from here."

"Well, I'll show you around quickly and then get outta your hair so you can rest."

Stepping in, we were in a foyer. It was quite spacious for the size of the house. I could imagine putting in a check-in desk here. You couldn't see much from here. On each side of the foyer were doorways that led to other parts of the house. One side lead down a hallway that I just knew already what I'd find.

"The primary bedroom is back that way, right?" I pointed to the doorway on the right.

"That's right."

Why was this place so familiar? I guess I had studied the pictures a few too many times.

Still in the foyer, I noticed a closet, then next to that was the doorway leading to the main living room. We stepped in. This was a large space. I could see into the dining room to the left and the kitchen was next to that. They weren't fully open to the living room, but more like separate rooms. I liked it.

"Some of this was added on after it was originally built, right? It wasn't always two stories, right?" I asked.

"Oh, I'm not sure." She opened the folder she was holding. "Um, I see nothing about that here, but you can probably check the public records at town hall. They have records going back seventy or eighty years, at least."

I made a mental note as we continued the tour.

"And up here is the attic. There are still a few things up there from the original owners, if you can believe that, but most were taken to the library years ago for safekeeping. Brenda, the librarian, would likely turn it over to you if you want it. Their names were James and Anna-Rose Collins. They had only lived here a few years before he was killed in what was believed to be a suicide, well that's one theory, anyway. Lots of rumors about what happened. She lived her until her death in the 1940s." She turned towards me, looking me up and down. "You know, you look a lot like her."

"Really? That's funny."

"Yeah, I have seen some pictures. Brenda has a few framed at the library. Anna-Rose loved the library and reading." She smiled. "Well, that's the tour. Any questions?"

"Not at the moment."

"Do you want me to show you where the hotel is?"

"Thanks, I think I can find it. Before I head over there, I'm going to take a few pictures and make a list." I smiled. "I appreciate you helping me with this and showing me around. I can't wait to start renovations."

"I think you'll love it here. Well, I'll get outta your hair. Again, welcome to Wisteria. I'll see you around town, and don't hesitate to reach out if you have questions or need help."

I walked her to the door; she dropped the key in my hand as she walked out. I smiled as I watched her climb into her car and head down the long, uneven driveway.

When she turned toward town, I shut the door, then turned around to take in the foyer. I could picture what this room could be. It would be beautiful.

"All mine." I threw my hands up as I spun around, taking it all in.

Then I noticed a bit of the wallpaper was peeling. I walked to it and pulled at it slightly. Gasping when I saw the paper underneath. I knew this pattern, but how? Hunter green leaves set between beige and gold stripes.

I tried to shake the feeling as I began walking through each room again. In my head, I added to my mental list of changes and updates. Drywall in all the rooms, fresh paint, new tiles, cabinets. I couldn't wait to get started.

The wallpaper in the foyer stayed in my mind as I walked back to it, pulling a bit more of the newer paper.

"Wow." An icy chill went through my body. "How do I know this paper?"

I couldn't place it as being visible in any of the pictures I had seen of the house. In fact, it wasn't obvious until I pulled back the top layer. Again, I was going to chalk this up to being overtired and way too familiar with the pictures of the house.

"Yeah, that's it."

For now, I'd head to the hotel, find food, and rest for the evening, in that order. I grabbed my purse from where I had dropped it on the floor when Linda and I first walked in.

I gave the house one more look before I climbed into my car. From the corner of my eye, movement in the attic window caused me to freeze. With my eyes, I doubled back to that spot.

Nothing. Yeah, I was tired. I rubbed my eyes and then drove toward town.

On my drive to the hotel, I took in the sights. My new hometown. It was a charming little place with tree-lined streets, crepe myrtles and roses blooming brightly in various hues of pink, red and white. Lush green lawns in front of craftsmen and ranch styled houses. No two of them are alike.

They all had a lot of character, not like the modern mini mansions in my old neighborhood. At the time, I loved my contemporary styled home with the straight lines. Looking back, it had a sterile, clinical feeling to it.

No, this differed completely from that.

"I love this place," I giggled.

A pulled onto Main Street. It seems every small-town has a street called Main. Here were various mom and pop shops with not a chain store in sight. I saw a couple of restaurants, a coffee shop, and a bakery.

"Oh, what a cute ice cream shop!" Sprinkles and Cream, how clever!

I couldn't wait to try a scope of homemade ice cream.

I passed a park where children were playing. Mothers watching nearby. A few people walked dogs. Smiles and waves as they passed each other. It was a perfect day to be out. Not too hot, sun shining, and a light breeze blowing.

I smiled, feeling at home and relaxed. My heart didn't ache like it had after losing my job and husband on the same day, and the heartache that followed coming to terms with both was healing. I could almost feel it going back together.

I pulled into the motor lodge. It was your typical motor lodge with about a dozen rooms. Pale pink stucco exterior with teal doors. Interesting choice, though a bit tacky, but somehow it worked.

I parked a few spots down from the office.

"Hi, welcome. Checking in?" The lady behind the desk greeted me with a smile. Her name badge read Molly.

She was probably my age, give or take a few years. Her hair was colored purple and black, cut short on one side and long on the other. It reminded me of the 80s punk. I loved it.

"Hi, yes, Lindsey Evans." I had taken my maiden name back. It just felt like I should.

"Ah, yes, I have you right here, Lindsey. You'll be here... Let's see... ah, for two weeks? Is that right?"

"Give or take. I just bought the Collins house and will start renovations. I'm not sure how long it will take for me to get it livable, at least enough for me to stay there."

"Oh exciting! That's a beautiful property, but in a haunting way." She said as she typed. "Good luck with it."

What did that mean? I smiled through my confusion.

She finished checking me in and activating my key card. "Alrighty, got you all set. Ice machine and vending machine are the door to the right, just outside the office. The diner across the street is the best for breakfast and they have a wonderful meat loaf. There is a deli at the opposite end of Main that has sandwiches, especially if you like roast beef and homemade chips. There is a new coffee shop, but they are only open from 6 a to 3 p." She thought for a second. "I'm sure you'll figure it all out. It's a small-town."

"Thanks, I probably will, but it helps to hear from a local."

"Been here my whole life. Stop by anytime. I'm happy to help ya out." She leaned forward onto the counter.

"Appreciate it, Molly. I'll keep that in mind."

After taking the key card, I headed down the covered walk towards my home for the next few weeks. I inserted the card and pushed the door open. The musty, stale smell of an unused room hit me. Looking around, it looked clean, at least just underutilized.

The decor inside was almost as tacky as the outside. Retro furniture set with almost a beach feel, but it missed the mark and just appeared gaudy. The walls were covered in sea foam, pinks, and teal swirls. The carpet was an aqua blue, and the bedspread was a striped pink and sea foam number.

"I love it!"

I squealed as I plopped on the rock-hard bed, then pulled out my phone to message my mom that I'd arrived. She would pass it on to the rest of the family.

With that done, I looked around once more as I thought about the last few months. I'd come a long way from that life. Married, working a dead-end job. Now I was in a new place, single, and about to embark on a wonderful adventure.

"Home."

Chapter Five: Anna-Rose (1882)

I had been living in Wisteria with James for about a month now. It was a wonderful month. I had gotten everything cleaned and polished. I sewed and hung curtains. Things to make it feel more like a home.

James suggested I order wallpaper to brighten up the house and make it feel like ours. I skimmed the catalog and picked a beautiful hunter green with yellow flowers and thick brown decorative lines running the length. It was going to be beautiful. He said he would hang it for me when it arrived. I couldn't wait.

The dull plaster walls of the clapboard house were plain. The bright colors and pattern on the wallpaper would make it feel like home.

I enjoyed the household chores more than I thought I would. Cooking was my favorite. I had learned many recipes and when I learned what supplies we had available; I could adjust.

James would hunt then smoke or salt the meat. This allowed us to have meat. Some of the game he caught differed from what I was used to, but it was delicious.

I had brought seeds with me to start a garden, but I hadn't yet done it with everything else I had going on and everything I was learning. However, I had picked up potatoes, onions, and other vegetables from the General Store and a few helpful neighbors.

We didn't yet have electric bulbs here, so I made candles and stored them. I had learned how to do this just before I left home. I had made several dozen. My first attempts didn't go well, but the last two dozen were beautiful, tapered and long burning. They hadn't traveled well, so I melted them down and reused the wax.

It was taking time, but we were finding our daily rhythm of life here as a married couple.

While I did my chores for the house, James worked in the field. He hadn't bought cattle yet. Though we had a milk cow, a few dozen chickens, a pair of mules, and a couple of pigs that would get nice and fat before the Fall, when they would be butchered for meat.

Instead of focusing on the other livestock, he wanted to first have crops in the ground so they would grow and be ready for Fall harvest, or so he hoped.

It was a lot of work for him to do alone. At the end of each day, he would come in exhausted, dirty, and starving.

Supper would be on the table the moment he was in the house.

"You are getting better at this, Anna-Rose." He smiled. He would eat every bite and then ask for second helpings.

After he ate, he would go outside to check the animals and our property once more. While he did that, I cleaned our supper. Then once we were both done, we would either sit up reading or I would sew.

I needed an entirely new wardrobe for this country life. I was thankful to have brought new bolts of fabric with me.

Other nights, he would be tired and suggest we turn in early, immediately after he came in from the nightly chores. He would expect me to submit to him, and I always did. I wanted to enjoy it but I didn't. It was awkward and painful. I thought perhaps we just needed to get comfortable with each other.

We were still relative strangers. I had only known him a few weeks before we married. My parents may have been correct. This may have been a mistake, at least so quickly.

I usually lay in bed after he'd fallen asleep and wonder when I would get used to it here. The sounds at night were both familiar and unfamiliar at the same time. Back home, we lived in a more urban area so there would be wagon wheels, rattling chains on the wagons, yelling voices and loud drunken singing most of the night. Mixed in would be dogs barking, the screech of an owl, and at times the howl of a coyote.

Here it was almost silent. You could hear the wind blowing through the trees, branches scratching against other branches, creaking and cracking as they swayed. There was also the howling of coyotes and wolves, far more than back home. They were likely packs of a dozen or so moving about. We had already lost a few chickens to them.

Then there were scratching and rustling sounds around the outside of the house. It could be an armadillo, a raccoon, or an opossum perhaps. There was always something scratching around. They would get in my scrap pile, but I didn't mind too much. I loved all the little critters.

I especially loved the crows that would visit. Their black feathers were so beautiful to me as I watched them soar and fly around the trees until they would settle. They would caw and bounce around on the branches. I would talk back to them and sometimes I'd throw out scraps just for them.

But at night, I hated having to use an outhouse. It had taken me some time to get comfortable taking a rifle and trudging through the dark with only a small oil lamp or candle to guide my way. James had laughed at my fear and belittled my feelings. I felt small and silly about it.

My first night here played through my mind.

"Oh, Anna-Rose, you are so naïve." He laughed. "Just go to the outhouse. You will be fine."

"But what about animals?"

"Take the rifle." He rolled his eyes.

"I don't know how to use one."

"You are such a child. Go use the outhouse. I'll be in bed." He stomped off. He stripped as he walked off. "And hurry up."

I internally laughed at myself now, though I was still cautious and scared. I could now go with little fuss.

Each Sunday, I attend church alone. James was not a churchgoer as he said, "That's for women, children, and old men."

I didn't mind too much. It was something I enjoyed and had done my entire life, so I would go now. I enjoyed the sermons, but my favorite part was singing the hymns. Singing was something I enjoyed, and I had been told I had a pleasant voice.

I immediately made friends with a few of the local women. My two closest friends were Dorothea and Leonora. Leonora was married with three young boys and Dorothea had recently gotten married.

They promised to teach me the things I needed to know, especially how to store foods.

"Leonora makes the best jams. She will teach you everything she knows." Dorothea said one day after church.

"Thank you, dear, but you make the best homemade pickled vegetables. If it can be pickled, Dorothea Louise can perfect it."

"I hope to learn from you both. This is my first time living like this. I mean on my own in the West."

"We are both happy to teach you. We have both grown up here."

Overall, I had had a good month as I adjusted to my new married life, far away from home and everything I knew. There had only been the few bumps as I learned the sounds, new skills, and learn my role in life. I looked forward to what this new life held for me.

Chapter Six: Lindsey (April Present Day)

I was stripping the wallpaper when I heard the crunch of gravel and the hum of a car pulling down the driveway. It had to be my dad and brother. They were due any minute. I put down the scoring tool and wiped my hands before heading outside to greet them.

They were both exciting the car and were stretching when I stepped out on the porch.

"Hello! Oh, so glad you made it."

"Hi, wow, Lindsey, this is stunning." Dad said, coming forward to hug me and then I moved to hug my brother, Bryan.

"Yeah, this is great." Bryan added.

"Thanks. It's going to take some work, but I can see the final product." I tapped my finger against my head. "Well, let me show you around."

We headed into the house so I could give them the grand tour, pointing out work I had already completed, and telling them my future plans. Most of what I had done so far was clean the years of dust and cobwebs, plus killed weeds that had grown up through the holes in some floorboards.

It was a pier and beam style home which allowed the weeds to grow up through the damaged floor. Luckily, replacing the boards had been something I could do by myself.

"This entire section here, as you can see, is new boards. It was nearly rotten out."

My brother toed a few boards. "Good work, sis."

"Thanks. I just need to finish sanding and staining so it all matches." I was extremely proud of all I had done, but I was still behind where I thought I'd be by the time they arrived. "Of course, the roof was another story. I had to find a roofing company, but they made quick work of it."

I was relieved that there hadn't been too much damage inside the house. Only in a few spots upstairs, but overall, it was in fair, fixable condition.

I'd gotten extremely lucky that the company had come out so quickly. I called on my second day here, and they came out the very next day.

"That's a small-town for you." Molly had said to me when I'd given her an update on my house.

In addition, I had cleared out all the old furniture, placing it in the barn for now. I didn't know yet what I would do with it. Most would likely be donated, but I could refurnish it and sell it.

One piece, a gorgeous club chair, felt familiar to me, almost like I had picked it out. But, obviously, I hadn't. That piece I hoped to recover, restore, and then use somewhere within the house.

It would probably go in my bedroom. I would decide on the rest once my furniture and things were out of storage. I knew I'd need all new furniture for the guest bedrooms and a new mattress for me. But until I got my stuff, I couldn't make a solid plan on the rest.

"Wow, Linds, this is really something. I can definitely see what you have in mind." Bryan commented as he scanned the living room.

"Thanks, I'm excited." I beamed with pride. "Well, do y'all want to get right to work, head over to the hotel, or get some lunch?"

"Y'all? You're one of them now." He teased.

I replied by punching him playfully in the arm.

"Children." Dad chuckled while teasingly scolding us. "I'd actually love to get lunch first, if you don't mind. After we can swing by the hotel to drop our bags and then we'll be happy to work the rest of the day."

"Great. I know just the place."

We headed over to the Wagon Wheel Diner. They offered yummy blue-plate specials I knew dad would love. He was always down for a good meal at a good price. His nickname was Frugal Phil. Yep, Ole Phillip Evans was a sucker for a deal.

But my lunch of choice was usually the Jerry #1 from Jerry's Sub shop. It was a tuna on a wheat roll with a thick tomato and fresh black pepper, a crunchy homemade pickle on the side, and homemade chips.

We ordered, then chatted about all the small talk things, family gossip, my new house, and their drive out from Virginia. They drove rather than fly so my dad could bring some of his favorite tools.

"I don't trust rented tools." He had told me on the phone when we had planned the trip. "I've been using mine for years."

While we visited, a few of the locals stopped by the table to say hi and ask how I was settling in. I introduced them to my dad and brother, though a few I only had met once.

I'd only been here a few days myself. But staying in the motel in town, I was close to the action of town.

"Everyone is so nice. I can see why you like it." Dad reached for my hand over the table.

"Yeah, everyone's been helpful and welcoming. I feel like I'm home." I smiled at dad.

"I'm so happy to hear. You've had a rough time of it recently."

"I never did like that guy," Bryan added.

"You didn't?"

"Yeah, he never seemed respectful. There was something slimy underneath that smile of his," Bryan said.

He'd said nothing before, so his admission caught me off guard. I had always thought Derek and I were soulmates, that we'd been happy together until maybe the past six months or so of our marriage.

Of course, the divorce had surprised me. Looking back, it was the right thing to do.

Thankfully, our server brought our food so we could focus on eating and less on this chit-chat about my ex-husband and my failures of late. This was my new start and adventure. I didn't want thoughts of my recent past haunting it.

After lunch, I drove them to the motor lodge and introduced them to Molly.

"We're so happy y'all are here. We haven't had this many people stayin' here since the last quilt festival."

I wasn't sure if she was joking or not. There were only the three of us. Could we really be a crowd? And what was a quilt festival? I guess I would find out in March when it was time for the festival again, as Molly confirmed for me.

With all the work that my new home needed, specifically the plumbing, I had to extend my stay at the fine Wisteria Motor Lodge. Molly assured me it was no problem. They wouldn't need the room for months.

"Not until the county fair in September."

It was April. I now had two festivals to look forward to. I wonder what else they did around here. Perhaps a Fourth of July picnic, town wide Halloween party, or a Christmas pageant. I couldn't wait to see all the small-town fun.

After dad and Bryan had their bags settled in their rooms, we stopped at the hardware store to grab some supplies and then went back to the house.

The plan was for dad and Bryan to work on the plumbing starting with the main bathroom.

"We should have this all replaced by tomorrow afternoon." Dad said as they unloaded supplies.

While they worked on getting the pipes in working order, I got back to the wallpaper. I had new wallpaper ordered that should arrive in a few days. I'd bought a vintage pattern as I wanted to reflect the house's original style and give a nod to the past owners.

There was still a ton of junk and old trunks in the attic. I hadn't gone through it yet but would soon. It wasn't a priority, but floors that I didn't fall through and running water that didn't leak all over the newly repaired floors were top on the list.

After a couple of hours, I heard a wonderful sound from down the hall.

"Is that running water?" I asked as I set down my scrapper and headed towards the bathroom.

"It is." My dad informed me. "We got all the pipes changed out. Most were rusted through."

"We also looked under the house. We'll need to replace more, to the other bathrooms and the kitchen, before we can say it is all good, but at least one bathroom is done." Bryan added.

"That's great. Thanks so much."

"We'll need to get more pipe tomorrow, once the hardware store is back open."

"What kind of town's hardware store closes at 5?" dad muttered.

"This town." I giggled. "I love it, and you get used to the business hours around here. Speaking of..." I checked the time. "If you want dinner, we need to get moving."

We started cleaning up. I had gotten all the wallpaper removed in the foyer and living room and had started in one hallway. It would have to wait until tomorrow.

Bryan and dad were loading their tools into the trunk of their car, and I was in the house alone, when I heard the boards behind me creak. I spun around to say something to either dad or Bryan, but nobody was there. I heard the creaking footsteps behind me again, so I turned in the other direction.

"Hello...? Bryan... okay, stop teasing me." I turned again, trying to find the source of the sound.

Creak, creak. An icy chill ran through me. I shivered as the sound was now right in the room with me. I spun around and around as it seemed to circle me.

The sound of heavy breathing came from my left and then my right, but I couldn't see anything. My heart was nearly beating out of my chest as the breathing sound got louder. An icy breeze blew over me.

Then the front door opened, and my brother strolled in. I launched myself into his arms.

"Are you okay? Did you see a mouse or something?" He chuckled.

"No, no… just the floorboards were creaking, and it was like someone was walking around me, circling me." My voice wavered as the fear choked me. "There was a breathing sound."

I was near tears and probably sounded insane, but I didn't care. That *freaked* me out, and I wasn't normally the easily scared type.

"Old homes creak and pop and make all kinds of noises. Remember Aunt Jackie and Uncle Sal's old house? It sounded awful. Almost like when Uncle Sal stood up, all the pops and cracks of his joints." He laughed.

"I know you're right, but… it just felt like someone or something was here."

I couldn't shake the feeling. It was almost like someone was watching me, even now. I rubbed my arms to try to get the chill out of my bones, even though it was a warm day.

He looked around. "Doesn't seem to be anyone here. And when did you get so jumpy?"

"I don't know." I shivered. "This is going to sound crazy, but it was almost like I could feel it deep in my soul, though."

"What? That's insane, Linds." But, despite his tone, he hugged me. "You're probably just tired. Let's go catch up to dad."

I nodded, and we went outside to join our father. As I climbed in the car, I looked back at the living room window just as a shadow crossed in front of it. It was almost like that first day I had been here.

A whisper of wind blew. "Anna-Rose."

Chapter Seven: Lindsey (April Present Day)

I bought an extra-large coffee from Jack's Beans this morning after sleeping fitfully last night. I couldn't get the sound of the creaks and that voice out of my mind. There was something about it that made my soul fearful and want to hide, but that was crazy.

There was no logical reason for my fear. That name meant almost nothing to me. Only that it was the name of the original owner.

From what some in town said, she had moved here around 1882 with her new husband. They lived here together for about two years before he died.

He'd been shot. But there were three versions to the who had done it. One theory was that he had killed himself, another was his wife was attached by wolves and he had accidentally got shot in the process of saving her. Then the last story was she had killed him. Obviously, there was nobody still alive that knew the actual story.

Linda had checked on me the day before dad and Bryan arrived. We had grabbed an ice cream from Sprinkles and Cream. She shared with me that her grandmother knew Anna-Rose.

When Edith, Linda's grandmother, had been born, Anna-Rose was forty-nine. As a young child, what Edith remembered was limited to seeing her at church and the few times she would grocery shop. Otherwise, she kept to herself. Late in her life, Anna-Rose hired high school girls to help her around her home.

"She'd helped Anna-Rose around the house and running errands for her. Anna-Rose confided in her losses. She had been pregnant a few times but lost the babies. It had been heartbreaking for her."

"How sad."

"My grandmother had been there when Anna-Rose was on her deathbed, as her circle had gotten small over the years." Linda frowned. "Grandmother said Anna-Rose shared she had, in fact, killed her husband. Honestly, I don't know if that's true. Ramblings of a dying woman. Maybe guilt over his death in general. Who knows?"

I found this fascinating. What if her husband's spirit was still here, waiting for her spirit to return? I wonder if she ever would.

"Earth to Lindsey." Bryan waved his hands in front of me.

"What? Sorry... What's up?" I tried to sound casual.

"Dad wants you to come look at the plumbing in the kitchen."

"Oh okay, coming."

I followed him from the bedroom where I had been scraping yet more wallpaper. This house was covered in what appeared to be never-ending wallpaper. I was only going to add new wallpaper in select rooms, like the foyer and maybe an accent wall in the living room. The rest of the house was going to get fresh drywall and paint.

Though there was a wall with shiplap that I was considering cleaning up and staining. I hadn't made that decision yet.

While I had experience doing drywall, I had already contacted a local company to do it for me. My dad and brother couldn't stay long enough to help with it, and I couldn't do it all by myself. I couldn't hold the drywall in place and also screw it in. I needed a second set of hands, at least.

"Oh good, so I wanted to show you some things here before I change the configuration." Dad said. He then explained how the current pipes were configured.

"It looks like someone used sub-par parts here and here. As we had already seen in the bathrooms, this house was just piece milled together as it evolved. I'm going to do the same upgrades in here, but I think while we're doing that, we can move the sink. Which is what I wanted to get your thoughts on?"

He walked to the far wall that had the window facing the backyard. Tape measure in hand, he pulled it out about five feet.

"I was thinking we could move everything here." He pointed to a spot under the window. "I've marked it on the floor. The sink would be right under the window here."

He'd laid out a grid on the floor with painter's tape. I looked around the entire kitchen area and could almost picture it.

Walking over to stand next to him, I looked at the yard, imagining myself right here washing dishes and watching the birds and squirrels. As I acted out washing dishes, a smile spread over my face.

"Yeah, yes, I'd like that."

"Great. We'll get things rearranged and the new plumbing run over here. It actually looks like it came over here once upon a time, so it should be easy enough."

They got back to work and so did I. I was loving how things were changing and coming together.

They stayed for another four days, which allowed us to get a lot done. The last day was spent replacing rotten boards in the walls to get it prepped for the new drywall that would be installed soon.

We also got all the plumbing and electrical updated. These were the two major things keeping from not living in my house, but with them done, I could make my plan to finally getting moved in.

"Hey, Molly!" I said as I entered the motel office.

"Oh, hey, Lindsey! How's the house comin' along?"

"It's good. I'm almost done. I have some drywallers in there today and I should be able to move in officially on Thursday, which is why I'm here."

"Wonderful, but we sure will miss you around here."

"Yes, I'll miss it too, but I'll see you around town, I'm sure."

"Definitely! Maybe we can grab lunch or coffee sometime." She said, as she typed away on the computer.

"I'd love that." I smiled. "I have been so busy on the house; I haven't met many people yet."

"Oh, I'll introduce you around more, too." She stopped typing and a printer behind her came to life. "Alrighty-roo, I'm just printing out a receipt. On Thursday, just drop me your keys anytime. I have no other guests, so no rush."

"Thanks so much." I took the paper from her and waved as I went out the door.

With that handled, I needed to call the storage place about my furniture. I had kept very little, but it would be enough to get me started until I had time to order what I needed for guests.

The house was the ideal place to run a bed-and-breakfast type of agritourism business. There was one bedroom that I was planning to use. It was the only one on the first floor and had a small room connected to it I assumed was meant as a nursery.

My idea was to use this smaller room as my office. It would make this downstairs hallway my private space. Guests would have use of the rest of the house.

This would leave the upstairs for guests. It had two large bathrooms and four bedrooms. While downstairs there was a half bath.

Then there was a formal dining and living room that would be make the perfect common spaces to share with guests. I could serve meals in the dining room and lay out board games for the guests to enjoy in the living room.

The entire upstairs didn't appear original to the house, but added at some point. As Linda had suggested, I could check public records. To do that, it would mean taking time away from the house and I really needed to get it to a more livable state first.

It was nearly the end of April and I wanted to have the house ready for guests by the end of May, so my focus remained on the house.

I had my website ready to go, but hadn't published it or started advertising. I would do that once I had a clearer idea on if the renovations were on schedule. So far, it was only a day or two off my target, but I think I could make up some of that time soon.

It was still in my plans to find out more about my house. So, once I got to a better stopping point, I would make a point to get out to city hall and also the library, as Linda had suggested.

I checked the time. I needed to get back to the house in case the drywallers hit a snag.

"But first, coffee."

The smell from Jack's Beans hit me from across the street. I looked both ways out of habit, but I only saw one car on the street, and it was going the other way. The bell above the door rang as I stepped inside.

"Hi, welcome back. Lindsey, right?" The dark-haired, gray-eyed man behind the counter said.

"Hi." I looked at his name badge. "Oh, I'm guess you are Jack from the sign."

He chuckled, "That's me. Jack's Beans."

"I love the coffee. Bree said you came up with the blend yourself." Bree was the employee that usually helped me, but she wasn't here now.

"Oh, yeah. I did some traveling a few years back. Learned quite a bit about coffee."

"Well, good job." I grinned. "Can I get a large drip?"

"Comin' right up." He flashed a dimpled smile as he grabbed a large cup and turned to get my coffee.

I tried not to stare or be completely goofy standing there waiting. I looked at the tchotchkes on the counter to distract my mind from the hottie behind it.

"Here ya go."

He smiled, setting it on the counter. He rang it up, announcing the total. I tapped my card and then grabbed my cup. I walked to the side table where the creamers and sweeteners were, but then turned back to him.

His face brightened, which caused me to get flustered, and I panicked. I almost had something clever to say and then it was gone.

"Um, thank you." I saluted with my cup and then hurried added cream and sugar, then clumsily backed out of the shop before I put my foot in my mouth.

"See ya around." He called as I stumbled out. I waved behind me.

Once back in my car, I giggled a bit. He was *cute*. I'd have to remember to go when he worked. I backed out of the parking spot and pointed the car home.

It wasn't a long drive and when I pulled up; I noticed the driveway was packed with work trucks, so I pulled off the drive to park under my favorite shady oak tree. It was the spot I would soon add picnic tables to. The tree branches created the perfect, cooling shade.

As I got out of the car, I glanced around. There were more workers than I thought would be here. I'd been thinking he would have sent maybe three or four workers, but this was a dozen or so.

"Oh, hey, Ms. Lindsey." The foreman, Greg said, pulling his cap off, wiping his forehead with the back of one hand and in the other, he held a clipboard. It looked like a work order.

"Hi, Greg. Wow, this is quite the operations you have going on."

"Yep. Gotta take care of our newest resident and business owner."

I placed my hand over my heart. "Aw, thank you, but I'm not a business owner yet."

"That's why I gotta get you up and running." He set down the clipboard on the back of his truck and grabbed a hard hat, handing it to me. "I got the paint samples for you. I had Marcus paint them onto the living room wall. Follow me."

I plopped the hat on my head. "Oof." The weight of it surprised me.

"You good?" Greg asked.

"Yeah, sorry, I wasn't expecting the weight on my head." I tapped the hat. "All set."

He nodded. I followed him through the foyer and around to the living room. Both rooms were complete and I could hear his men working upstairs. Did that mean that the entire downstairs was done?

"Your guys sure have gotten a lot done already."

"Yeah, they are making quick work of everything. They're upstairs now." He turned towards the stripes of paint on the wall. "Now here are the ideas you gave me."

He named them from left to right. "This is the White Truffle. This one is Alpaca. Sea salt, Grey Owl, and finally Repose Gray."

I studied each. The White Truffle was nice, but it had more of a pink hue than I'd expected or wanted, so that one was out. The Alpaca had a warm feeling about it, plus I liked the name.

I could picture guests asking the color and I'd tell them Alpaca with a giggle. They would love it and give me five-star reviews on Yelp. At least, that was my daydream version.

Of course, the Grey Owl could get the same response and it had a nice soothing effect on me. It would make me think of the owl that lives in the backyard. I hadn't gotten a good look at it yet, but if I had to guess, it was either a barn owl or a spotted owl. I was no expert.

"Okay, the Sea Salt in the main rooms and the Grey Owl in the bedrooms and bathrooms."

"Perfect. Then you want the white trim on everything else, right? Stain on the cabinets in the kitchen and all the bathrooms?"

"Yes, that works." My body tingled with excitement as I pictured everything complete. It was all coming together.

"I'll run down to the hardware store right now so I can get the guys started on it."

I moved into the kitchen. My project for today was to install the backsplash. I had a two-by-two-inch stone tiles to add as a backsplash. It was an off-white color and with the beige hue of the Sea Salt on the walls, along with the dark walnut-colored cabinets. It should look good in here.

I worked quickly to keep ahead of the workers. Luckily, I got the last section in place, as they came in to sand and prep both the walls and cabinets to be painted. I moved out to the barn to get it in shape so I could get animals soon.

I worked for a few hours on the barnyard fence. I knew I wanted to get pigs and would need a sturdy fence for that. There was a time when I was on my aunt and uncle's farm. The pigs crashed right through the fence.

We spent an hour chasing and getting them back in the pen. Then Uncle Sal and I worked to reinforce the fence.

"Remember this, Linds. If you ever have pigs, they like to barrel through barriers. They're stubborn, so make sure you have a sturdy fence."

I mumbled to myself now, "I remember, Uncle Sal."

He had been gone for nearly ten years now. I often wonder what he would say about my life today. Aunt Jackie was now in a nursing home. Her memory was spotty, but I still called her every Sunday.

At the end of the day, the walls were dry walled and ready to be painted. The workers had all gone with a promise of being back in the morning to do the painting.

I stood in the newly remodeled kitchen. The cabinets were perfectly laid out, and the tiles looked wonderful.

My project for tomorrow was to work on more of the outdoor spaces by putting together the picnic tables. I saved about fifty dollars a piece by having them shipped unassembled. I'm sure I would curse my cheap self for that tomorrow as I got them put together, but it saved me.

I walked through the house to do a visual inspection of each room, soaking in the beauty of it all.

"This is mine. All mine." I spun around and around in my new bedroom. I could picture where each piece of my furniture would go in here.

I inhaled and then grabbed my keys. Just three more nights in the motel and then I'd be home.

"So much still to do."

There was a whisper of sound to my right, then it felt as if someone grabbed at my hand. I pulled back, looking around. There wasn't anything. I wasn't normally one with an overactive imagination, but these weird sounds, the strange sensations, were all too much.

The quicker I finished this house and had other people in it, the better. I thought as I ran out of the house.

Chapter Eight: Anna-Rose (1882)

I stood scraping and washing the dishes at the sink as I glanced out the kitchen window. James had installed a water pump right in the kitchen for me and placed it by this pane glass window. Not all farmhouses in the area had glass or a water pump right in the kitchen, though we'd had it in Virginia.

This was the best spot to look out at the barn and part of the fields where James worked. At times, I would catch a glimpse of him, and I'd smile.

He was trying to finish getting the crops in the ground and then would travel to buy cattle and other livestock for us. We already had two milk cows and a few dozen chickens. Most we got eggs from, but I would butcher one as needed for meals.

We also had a few pigs that would be slaughtered in the Fall, so I fed them well each day. They were messy but friendly creatures. James had warned me to not to get attached to any of them, because they would be on our dinner plate one day.

I understood, but I still enjoyed them all.

I had been here three months now, and we were slowly getting to know each other and fall into a daily routine. The most troublesome part was still in the bedroom.

I wanted to enjoy this time with my husband the way Maribeth did. She made it sound marvelous. I know it was wrong to think this way, but the feelings of love I had for him, I wanted to bring into our bed.

I guess our mothers had been right. It was something women endured and were only enjoyed by the men, and I supposed some women.

"Anna-Rose? Where are you?" He hollered even before he was inside the house.

"Here." I yelled out to James.

He stomped into the kitchen. His eyes were wide, and his nostrils flared.

"You're still cleaning from breakfast. I thought you would have dinner prepared by now." He advanced on me, anger just below the surface.

"It nearly is. These dishes are from my preparations." My voice wavered.

I had not seen him angry like this before. It was confusing and scary. He had seemed pleasant this morning. Were the pressures of running our farm wearing on him?

"Good. Don't make me wait for a meal, *ever*." He growled.

"I... I won't." I took a step back. His tone petrified and confused me. "I just need to get it on the plate."

He nodded and walked out of the room. I heard him go to the outside water pump to wash up, and then the sounds of the pump moving up and down.

I wasn't able to see it from here, so I hurriedly pulled the stew from the oven, got plates, and served a hefty portion on to James' plate. I set it at his place at the table with a large slice of freshly baked bread.

Whatever caused his angry mood, I didn't want to make it worse.

He stomped back in, plopping hard into his chair without a word. He got right to the business of eating. The tension coming off of him was heavy and unsettling. As I watched him with my head lowered, my nerves were pulsing under the skin. I kept my head down as I ate my food without a word. No reason to further fuel his flame.

When he had finished his first serving, he looked at me and then at his plate. When I didn't move, he cleared his throat, so I scurried over to grab his place, serving him another large portion. He inhaled the second portion, nodded, and left the house.

I wept quietly over my food after his departure. That was upsetting. Just when I thought I was getting used to being married and living with a man, I realized I didn't understand him at all.

I scraped my food into the bucket for the pigs and cleaned up our meal. I then went to check on the laundry that I'd put out this morning. It was dry, so I took it off the line and brought it in, prepping it to be ironed.

Once all those chores were complete, I immediately started on supper. Whatever had been wrong with him earlier, I wanted to avoid this evening. I would do everything in my power not to upset him.

His mood only seemed to have multiplied by the time he marched in at sunset.

"Supper. Now." He snarled as he plopped in his chair.

I placed the plate of fried pork, onions, and potatoes in front of him. I'd piled it high.

"Drink."

"Oh, of course." I brought him a glass of water from the sink. My hands were shaking so badly I could barely hold the cup. As I was setting the glass in front of him, a small amount splashed out.

He launched out of his chair and grabbed me hard. It startled me so badly that I felt like all the air was sucked out of me.

"What do you think you're doing? Did you try to spill that on me?"

"No, of course not. It was an accident." I stammered out.

He squeezed my arms harder and pulled my face within an inch of his. His eyes flamed and a vein in his forehead pulsed. How could a splash of water make him this furious?

"You cannot be that incompetent! Get it cleaned up. Now!"

He let go, pushing me hard away from him. I grabbed a towel and wiped the teaspoon amount of water, then scurried to my chair without a word. My throat had a lump in it the size of Texas. There was no way I was going to be able to eat now.

On the other hand, he devoured his food and slammed his fist on the table to demand more. This was not the James I fell in love with. The tension coming from him would have a Texas Ranger running for the hills.

After he had eaten his fill, he stomped out to do his evening chores. It was only when he was away that I could fall apart. I let the heavy tears fall as I stared at his now empty chair.

Unfortunately, I only had a few moments to wallow in my sorrow, because I had to get supper cleaned before he came back. He would expect us to go to bed shortly after he came back in, as he worked so late into the evenings and had to be up early for morning chores.

My stomach twisted at the thought of what awaited me once we were in our bedroom. Even after being married for several months now, I didn't enjoy the *duties*. I couldn't think of them as anything else but a cruel punishment for something and an obligation to please him.

But he didn't seem to enjoy it any more than I did. He was rough and uncaring, pushing away from me the minute it was over. He'd roll to his side facing the wall and would immediately fall asleep.

I thought with time, I would get used to it, and we would learn to love each other more deeply. Instead, it felt like the longer we were married, the more his temper grew and the less I loved him.

I was nearly done with the clean-up when I heard his heavy boots leading towards the house. I quickly shoved the last of the unwashed items under a towel and then dried my hands on another, hoping he wouldn't notice.

"You finished?" He growled.

"Yes."

"Bed. Now."

"Of course." My stomach churned, and a lump reformed in my throat.

After he was done, he rolled off of me to his side of the bed, facing the wall, like always. I laid there in pain and agony, both physically and emotionally, letting the quiet tears slide down my face as the sorrow washed over me.

I hate him.

Chapter Nine: Lindsey (May Present Day)

I'd been in the house a week now, and it felt like I was finally home. I woke each day with a smile as I stepped out on my porch with a warm mug of coffee to watch the sun come up. This was the best view. I couldn't wait for my first guests to enjoy this moment too.

I sat on my new porch swing to enjoy the morning and reflect on my new life. After getting my stuff out of storage and set up in the house, I realized how much I needed. To finish it out, I had gone shopping in Waco, as that was the closest furniture store. I ordered a new mattress for myself, a kitchen table, and a completely new living room set.

In addition, I bought complete bedroom sets for all four guest bedrooms. As I had planned, I would set two up with queen beds and the other two with two twin beds each. I was advertising as family friendly. With my set up, I could have two families at the same time. It would be delivered next week.

It put a hefty dent in my savings, but it was worth it. Though technically, I had budgeted for this.

The place was going to be perfect. I already had the first month booked solid, and then random days booked after that.

Simone had helped me set up my marketing. She wasn't only my best friend, but she was a marketing genius. She was the Vice President of marketing at her tech company.

"But I'm bored with this job. I need a challenge. Something new." She'd told me while we were discussing the strategy for my business.

"Well, you're helping me. That's something new, right?"

"Oh, sis, this is easy stuff. I could market the heck out of your place in my sleep. No, I mean something completely new."

"What are you talking about?"

"I'm talking about, I'm looking for a new job. I'm resigning from my job."

"What? You loved that job. You'd waited so long for it."

"I know. I know, but you know me. I'm always chasing the next big thing."

That's true, I'd known here nearly ten years, and she was never happy with today. She had to have more or new.

"Well, good luck. You know I have your back." I smiled at her image on the phone. "Now, back to my website. Do you like this color?"

We continued to create my brand, then publish my site. She had me create ads on the various social media sites. It was working because within minutes I had visits to my site and within a few hours I had my first booking.

I watched my analytics report as visitor after visitor came to my site.

"This is happening!" I'd giggled to myself.

As I sipped my coffee, I contemplated what to do with my day. I needed to go to the General Store, bread, milk, eggs, some veggies.

I've been trying out a few new recipes that I hoped to perfect. While I was a good home cook, I wanted to get better as a bed-and-breakfast host. That meant I had been studying recipes and reading cookbooks.

I also had studied for and passed my food handler's certification, so that was just another box checked. It had opened the possibly to offer food, which I really wanted to do and was a huge part of my business plan.

There was still work to do around here, but I wanted to give myself a break from that. There was still plenty of time to get it all done before my first guests would arrive.

Once the sun was up, I took my coffee back into the house, rinsed my mug, then went to get showered and dressed for the day. I was putting my hair up in a high ponytail when I heard banging upstairs. It was almost like drawers opening and closing. The problem was, there weren't any drawers up there to open and close.

"What the —?" I turned to go upstairs when I heard footsteps moving down them. I grabbed my hairbrush from the counter before creeping down the hall to find out what that sound was.

The sound of the footsteps got louder, echoing through the house. I snuck down the hallway to the living room as quietly. Goosebumps raised as I turned the corner into the foyer. The stairs were to my right, but looking up, I saw nothing.

What had caused the sound?

I looked behind me into the living room, wanting to call out, but I couldn't form words or even a sound. My throat had gone completely dry.

I stood perfectly still, barely letting myself breathe as I listened. But after several minutes, I didn't hear it again. I exhaled heavily.

"I am not going to live in fear of something that may or may not be here." I stomped my foot.

Though my words and foot were brave, I didn't actually feel quite that courageous. My body said pack my things and back to Cali, but that would not happen. I shook off the paranoia and finished putting myself together to head into town.

Town was close enough that I could probably walk, but I would be carrying supplies back so car it was. Additionally, it was a warm day too, and I hadn't yet gotten used to the weather here. It was much hotter than I was used to by at least ten to fifteen degrees, which may not seem like much, but it had a higher humidity level, making it feel sticky.

I fanned myself and turned my A/C up in the car, then headed down my long driveway. I caught my house in the rearview and smiled. It was a beautiful house.

I had painted the outside a grayish blue with white trim. The roof was gray metal. I couldn't wait for the first rainstorm. The sound was going to be wonderful.

As I turned on to Main Street, a peace came over me. This was the right move for me, and I knew it. I slide my car into a spot near the General Store.

Stepping out of the car, I was immediately hit with the wonderful smell of coffee coming from across the street from Jack's Beans. It called to me like a siren's call.

I looked both ways and then made my way across the street. The bell above the door rang as I walked in.

"Hey Lindsey." Bree called from behind the counter.

She was close to my age, upper 30s or early 40s. Though I was a bad at judging people's ages. Still, maybe she was someone I could befriend. We had only spoken when I'd come in for coffee. But I wanted to make some friends in town.

My eyes shifted around, but no Jack. Darn, the guy was cute, and I had hoped to see him again.

"Hi, Bree. How's it going today?"

"Livin' the dream." She smiled, gesturing around her. "I love working here."

"I would too." I smiled.

"Large drip?" She asked.

"I guess I've been coming here a few times."

"Maybe once or twice." She laughed, then to turned to make my coffee.

"I'd also like to get a pound of the house blend." I picked up the sack from the display next to the register. She nodded, then turned to dispense the coffee. As it poured into the cup, the strong, bitter aroma filled the air. She slipped a drink sleeve around it and passed it over the counter with a smile. Then rang up the sale. I tapped my card, adding a tip of a few bucks.

"Thanks so much, Bree."

"And, thanks to you."

I hesitated as I tried to think of a way to ask her if she wanted to be friends. I felt like I was a child on a playground. Instead, I went to the side counter, adding creamer and sweetener, then grabbed a napkin, offered one last smile, before hurrying out of the shop.

As I walked back across the street, I berated myself for not talking to her.

"I need to make some friends. Why didn't I ask her?"

Because I wasn't a pig-tailed 6-year-old that wanted to play hopscotch. I was trying to build a business and a new life here. There would be time for friends soon. I mean, at least Molly seemed like she wanted to be friends.

I stood outside of the General Store, trying to decide if I would shop now or if I wanted to run down to the library. Linda had told me that Brenda at the library had the journals and pictures from Anna-Rose's house.

Maybe I should stop by to introduce myself and also ask if I could at least see them.

Plus, with the creaky and footsteps, it would be nice to understand more about what I may have gotten myself into.

I put my bag of coffee in the passenger seat, then walked down the block towards the library. I tried to imagine the town back when Anna-Rose walked these streets. Were they dirt roads back then? What would happen when it rained? Did they have wooden sidewalks like I'd seen on television shows? Did she take a wagon to town, or did she walk?

A lady passed me, greeting me with a hello and a how are you? I returned the greeting but continued on my walk.

I reached the library a moment later. It was a two story, all brick building with wide windows in front. They had decorated the windows for summer with fun beachy reads for both children and adult readers. It looked welcoming.

I stepped in, noticing with a smile all the familiar standards of a library. It immediately took me back to my favorite day in school, library day. The smell and row after row of neatly lined up books. The strategically placed tables and chairs for browsing your finds.

I scanned the room; it went back further than I thought from the street. I couldn't even see the back wall from here, and there was a staircase to my left.

I stuck my head around to see up it. It was narrow and dark.

"Helllooo." A lady with a short, permed hairstyle came from behind a shelf.

Taking her all in, she had that loving grandmother vibe, but your fun grandmother with her leopard print leggings and her bright red tank top with the word blessed scrolled across it. "Oh, are you Lindsey?"

"I am. Are you Brenda?"

"I am." She smiled brightly. "Are you here for Anna-Rose's things?"

"Well," I wasn't expecting her to offer them to me. I simply wanted to see them. "I don't know. Maybe I could just look at the journals."

"Oh, sure." She gestured me toward the stairs. "You know, dear, you look a lot like her."

"I keep hearing that. I'd love to see a picture of her."

"I have all of them."

We made it to the second floor. It was laid out like a museum, which I was not expecting. I thought we were going to a storage room. There were pictures, clothing items, and farming equipment in glass displays and on tables. The upstairs was broken down into rooms. I wonder what each represented. Maybe she would explain. But for now, I would listen and observe.

"This is the history of the town. I am the third caretaker and soon I'll be passing it on."

"Oh?"

"Yeah, my granddaughter is fifteen and has a genuine interest in this. She comes every day after school to help me."

"That's nice." I smiled. "It sounds like a fun after-school job, and what a wonderful time with your granddaughter."

"Yes, we both enjoy it." She walked to the far wall in a corner. "Here is the earliest picture we have of Anna-Rose. Isn't she lovely?"

I gasped as my eyes stared back at me from the faded monochrome photo. Even though she wasn't smiling, I knew if she was, it would be my smile. She was younger than I am now in this picture.

"See? She looks *just* like you," Brenda said with pride.

"She does. Wow! I know you told me, but seeing her... it's startling."

"I have more of her. In fact, I have a wall in here with things that were hers, more pictures, and a couple of her favorite recipes."

"Oh, really?"

I followed her into another room or section of the museum. I stepped to the wall that Brenda pointed to. It was covered, as she said, with all kinds of pictures and items.

"What's this?" I pointed to the contraption. All I could tell is it was old. It had prongs like a comb but was larger and shaped in a way that would make it difficult to brush one's hair.

"Oh, that's a cake breaker. They don't really make these anymore, but they are great for cutting spongy cakes, like angel food. This one is quite gorgeous. She was known for her cakes. Always donating them to church functions or school fundraisers."

"That's amazing."

"Yeah, and this was her famous chocolate cake. She shared it with the museum before she passed. In fact, she had called my grandmother, who was the curator at the time, and Anna-Rose worked with her catalog all of these items." She grinned. "Few people know that."

"That's amazing."

I looked at each item, fighting the urge to touch them. I read the recipes. I stared at pictures. Anna-Rose as a young woman. Anna-Rose at perhaps my current age, then as an elder woman. She was thinner than me. I had an extra thirty pounds, but otherwise, we looked so much alike.

There was a chime sound.

"Oh, that's for me. I will be right back. Feel free to look around."

She headed toward the stairs again. I stood there for a moment, digesting the information on display. I took a deep breath and began browsing the items again.

After I'd seen everything about Anna-Rose, I looked at other historic figures. I got halfway around the room when an article caught my eye. It was about James Collins.

It stated that Mr. Collins had been shot in an accident on their property. Anna-Rose had gone to the outhouse and was attacked by wolves. He came to help and was shot by mistake in the scuffle and then their cattle stampeded. It noted how distraught she was.

I gasped and read it again.

"Heartbreaking, right?" Brenda said from behind me.

"It really is. They weren't married long."

"Long enough, from what I hear."

"What do you mean?"

"He beat the heck out of her. I mean, obviously I wasn't there, but that was what everyone said."

I loved how people here always said things as if they were fact, but then added, 'that's what everyone said.' Did that make it a fact rather than just gossip?

"That's so sad."

"Well, do you want the journals while you are here? I have them just back here in a storeroom."

I followed her to the back of the building and through an ornate wooden door. The room was large and stuffed full of shelves overflowing with storage bins and boxes. She went right to one with a label of Collins on it.

"Here you go."

"Oof." It was heavier than I thought. "Thanks!"

"Well, stop by anytime at all. You are always welcome here, and once you get your business up and running, I would love to have to pictures to add to our museum."

"Oh, wow, that would be awesome. I will bring you one or two soon."

I took the heavy box the three blocks back to my car. I was sweaty and winded by then, but I still needed to go grocery shop.

I heaved a sigh, pulled out my list, and headed into get through it. The sooner I got it done, the sooner I could get home and dive into the journals.

Chapter Ten: Lindsey (May Present Day)

The journals turned out to be wildly fascinating. The author's handwriting was beautiful and scrolling. I could stare at it forever, as I read page after page of her hopes and dreams, then her love and excitement in those early months of marriage. I got to the part where his temper came out and had to close it.

A few tears escaped. Her confusion and sorrow came through the pages from years ago.

After reading a bit from her journals, I decided it was time to see what was left in the attic. I had only gotten a quick peek when Linda was showing me around. It had been dark, and I hadn't been up there since. It hadn't been a priority with all the other projects around the house. I mean, having a livable space seemed more important than dusty clothes and books.

I took two large contractor bags, a broom, gloves, and a rake because you just didn't know what I would need. The stairway leading up was airless; I sucked for air as I climbed the narrow stairs. I flipped the switch to the single light bulb. Nothing. Click, click. Still nothing.

"Crap, I should have brought a flashlight." I mumbled.

I peeked into the room. There seemed to be enough light coming from the lone window in the far corner and then coming up from the stairway. Maybe I could at least get started, then I could run back down later for a flashlight.

I started with a stack of old crates nearest the stairs. They were interesting, with their rusty latches and intricate hinges. Maybe I could clean them up and use them for storing extra blankets and sheets for the guest rooms. They could pull double duty as decoration and function.

I opened the first to discover a lot of dust and nothingness. The next had some old tin plates and bowls. Plus, a few ceramic figurines. I picked up one of the delicate ladies. She was dressed in a pink ball gown.

"I love it."

I would have to find a spot to display her. After setting it down, I moved to the next. This one was full of old, what looked to be old men's clothing.

"This is like straight of Little House on the Prairie." I held up a blue button-down cotton shirt.

"Anna-Rose!" a male voice yelled from somewhere below me, and then footsteps stomped around.

I jumped, throwing the shirt I'd just picked up. It disappeared into the darkness.

"Who's there?" I called down.

"Anna-Rose." The ghastly voice called out again.

The blood felt as if it rushed out of me at the sound. I grabbed the broom I'd brought upstairs with me and cautiously climbed down the stairs. Broom clutched tightly against my body. It would be a shield and weapon if needed.

"Hello. Is someone here?"

No one answered. The house was silent.

I walked through each of the upstairs rooms. Nothing. No evidence of anyone here. I headed downstairs, my heart pounding nearly out of my chest. After a quick scan of each room, I was sure I was going crazy. I didn't hear the voice or footsteps any longer.

I exhaled.

"I need to get a dog or finish this place up quickly, so it will be full of people." I set the broom in a kitchen corner and then I leaned against the sink.

"What just happened?" I blew out air. "Where's my flashlight?"

I didn't have a ton of things, but I don't remember seeing a flashlight in what I'd already unpacked. I pushed off from the sink and headed straight for the only two boxes I had yet to unpack. Of course, that's where it was.

Click, click. Dead batteries.

"Damn it!"

I knew without looking that I was completely out of batteries, which would mean a trip to the hardware store was in order. There was no way I was going back into that attic without additional light.

"So, now what to do with my day?"

I looked out the window. Garden it is. I'd already laid out the stakes for where I would put it. It was early in the summer, which was the perfect time to plant corn, cucumbers, melons, and tomatoes. I also had a few different types of peppers. It would just be a few rows or so of each to get started.

The ultimate plan was to have a quarter of an acre as my garden. It would be large enough to use for educational purposes with guests and also allow for filling my pantry. What I couldn't or didn't grow, I could always buy from other local farms.

I had starts for some, others I would plant from seeds. I headed toward the barn and storage area to grab the shovel and the first set of plants. Tomatoes first.

A couple of hours later, I was covered in sweat and dirt, but all my new plant babies were in the ground. I looked at them with pride. I pulled the hose over to give them a quick drink.

"Grow strong, little ones."

I put everything away, then stomped and shook off as much dirt as I could before heading straight to the shower. I striped as a made my way to the bathroom, depositing my clothes into the dark wicker hamper. Then turned on the hot water and stood waiting for it to heat.

Thankfully, my dad and brother did a wonderful job updating the plumbing, so it knew it wouldn't take long

I ran my hand under the water to test it. Perfect. I climbed under the scalding water, moaning when it hit me. My muscles had gotten quite a workout from the gardening. Squatting, lifting, digging. All my muscles had been worked, but it felt good.

I let the water run down my body as I felt the dirt, grime, and stress melt away. Actually, I had very little stress these days, except getting this old house in shape so I could get my business up and running. I couldn't wait.

I lathered up my hair, then soaped up with my new vanilla soap. A local business sold them at the farmer's market, which was held twice a month. I was hoping to use their product to stock my guest rooms.

A muffled voice called out.

"Anna-Rose, where are you?"

I froze. It was the same voice as before. Despite the scalding water, my skin went instantly cold. I quickly rinsed away the last of the soap, turned the water off, and grabbed my towel.

"Anna-Rose, where's my dinner?" There was a pause, and I heard the floorboards creak. "Answer me!"

It sounded like the voice was moving around the kitchen area. I crept down the hallway, wrapped in my towel. I was trying to be silent in my pursuit of the sound. If someone was here, I didn't want to get caught naked, and yet here I was naked and looking for whoever it was.

"There you are!" the voice said. It sounded like it was right in front of me, but I couldn't see anything, just a blurry fog.

Suddenly, the cold fog engulfed me, and I felt a chill clear to my soul. It was like I couldn't breathe. I gasped and struggled to catch my breath.

The shadow was all around me. I couldn't see beyond it. My heart thumped harder, but the rest of me was numb. I tried to fight but couldn't move a muscle. I stood there, wrapped in a towel, surrounded by a strange, dense cloud.

"Where's my dinner? Where is it, Anna-Rose?" The voice demanded.

I tried to respond, but the cold grow more intense, like it was suffocating me. I was frozen to that spot, unable to speak or move.

"Help." I tried to call out. "Help me." But it was barely above a whisper.

"No one will help you. You belong to me. *Never* forget that."

Then the fog lifted, and I collapsed to the floor, desperately sucking in air, trying to catch my breath.

"What was that?" I panted.

I laid there for several moments as I let my breathing normalize, and my heart to slow to a normal place. I tried to process what had happened.

"That was freaky." Finally, I rolled onto my back, still wrapped in the towel. I looked around but didn't see or hear anything. "I need to get a dog."

Chapter Eleven: Anna-Rose (1882)

I was working in my vegetable garden, enjoying the sun. It had been rainy and cloudy all week, so the warmth felt good on my face. I tilted my head to soak it up.

The harvest was going well. Potatoes, onions, tomatoes, carrots could all be put away for winter. Plus, I would start canning tomorrow.

James was away for a week or two. He wasn't sure when he'd be back. He had traveled to Fort Worth to buy cattle and get supplies we couldn't get here in Wisteria. I asked for nothing for me, only things that I could show were for the household. There was nothing I needed.

"No bolts of fabric?" He had asked me.

"No, my dresses are fine."

He had simply nodded and walked away.

I was going to cherish each minute of his absence to rest my body and soul. His temper had grown by the day. He never apologized exactly, but he mentioned his stress at starting this homestead. The cost of starting out and having nothing.

"I have to do it all by myself." He huffed.

"You are doing wonderfully." I whispered, adding a smile.

"I work darn hard around it." He slammed his fist down.

I didn't bother to reply. It seemed he simply wanted to talk it out, so I let him. Instead, I nodded or mumbled oh after some of his statements.

I tried to be understanding, but if he loved me, as he claimed, why take out those struggles on me?

My one joy each week was Sunday service. We had a wonderful pastor, and it gave me time to spend with my friends in town. Dorothea and Leonora were angels on earth. When I had questions about anything to do with running a household, they were more than happy to help.

Dorothea even came to my house to demonstrate storing and canning. It was something I'd never done before.

Even though he had been tentative about letting me have friends, ultimately, he enjoyed the benefits of it and allowed it.

"If it means that you will get better at caring for the household and not slacking behind every day, I am all for it. But if they impede your duties, no more friends." His stone-cold tone had me straightening my spine.

I hated he thought I wasn't pulling my weight around here. I worked daily in this house between the cooking and the cleaning, and then all the animals. We had two milk cows, chickens, and pigs that were my sole responsibility now. He only cared for the mules and the horse.

I patched his clothing and sewed him new clothing as needed. While I didn't get new things myself, I could patch when necessary. He came first in everything I did.

But I didn't argue. It wasn't worth it, and perhaps I could do better. His expectations for me were clearly higher and I would need to do more.

But for the next week, maybe two, I wouldn't have to live in fear of him and I could simply enjoy the moments of living in this beautiful part of the world. Living at my own pace with my own expectations.

After I harvested and cleaned the beds, I dug my shovel into the soft earth and turned it to add more seeds. I repeated the process, smiling as I did. When I was finished, I brought bucket after bucket of water to slowly water the seeds. Then I leaned against the fence and stared at my work.

I was proud of all my hard work, and without James here to worry about, I could pace my day the way I wanted to. I had my own schedule. Eating when I wanted, sleeping when I wanted, and doing the chores in the order that I wanted to do them.

At church on Sunday, the pastor spoke about marriage. He quoted from the bible. The direct verse he used was about wives submitting to their husbands. Knowing the bible as I did, he left off the part about husbands love their wives and to not be harsh with them.

Or the part about how a man should love his wife as he loves his own body. Perhaps I didn't understand it as I should because the pastor focused only on what the wife was to do for the husband.

Hearing this put an exclamation point on how I felt about James's anger being my fault. My stomach instantly twisted, and I squirmed in my seat as I realized I must be causing my own issues. Logically, I knew it wasn't true. I did everything as expected. He wanted a clean house, food ready on time, and a submissive wife. I did all of those things plus more.

I straightened my spine as I set my mind to do even more and do it better. Though that didn't absolve James of his responsibility in all of this. He had to do his part as well.

I'd been raised with loving parents though they weren't overall affectionate with each other, nor to me. But they were patient and kind to each other. It was rare for there to be a raised voice.

Though my father had a firm tone at times, especially when I told him I was going to marry James. I don't regret my decision, but there were times I think my parents may have been right that I didn't know him well and it was too fast.

When I'd met James, I thought we had that and more. He was affectionate, something I wasn't accustomed to, but almost craved. So, when he turned his charms and affection my way, I was hooked.

And just like a fish, reeled in, and trapped for life.

My belief was until death parts us so we would have to overcome these things and find our way back to the way things were in Virginia. Happy and in love.

The final hymn was sung, and the pastor's final prayer said, then the service was over. I grabbed my picnic basket and blanket from the back of the church, then joined my friends and their families for a picnic.

I spread out the blanket near Leonora's. It was her husband and their three young boys, though at the moment Emmett was talking with a group of men about the cost of cattle.

My ears perked as I wanted to know more. It might come in handy when James got back if we could talk about his troubles.

"Can you believe the cost of cattle right now?" Emmett asked.

"Yeah, I was lucky enough to sell mine for $25 a head." The gentleman said.

"That's a decent price in this market."

As I was listening, Leonora interpreted, so I didn't get to hear more about what the men were discussing. It looked like it got heated after that.

"When does James return?"

"End of the week, I believe." I honestly had no idea, but that's when I expected him.

"Oh, that's wonderful. Are you all going to have children soon?"

She looked at her youngest, who was toddling around us, while the other two ran in circles. The little one was trying to keep up with the older children. He squealed a bit when he couldn't get near them.

"I don't know. It is difficult to plan these things, isn't it?" I laughed lightly. Truth was I was counting my cycle days now to determine if I could be.

"Don't I know that?"

She continued unpacking her family's feast, while I had my simple bread with ham and an ear of corn that I'd roasted last night. Then I had some freshly sliced melon from the garden. It wasn't much, but I needed little. It was just me. I enjoyed the simple things.

As the sun moved across the sky, I mostly listened to the families and friends around me chat, mingle, and fellowship. It was the perfect way to end the day.

After it was over, I hugged my two friends and then made the long walk from town back to our homestead. I didn't mind the walk. It was a gorgeous day, and I had no chores waiting, except to feed the animals. I picked some wild berries on my way. They would make a nice pie or perhaps I could make some jam.

I was so thankful for the peace of not having more responsibilities now. It meant I could savor this moment. The quiet breeze, the chirp of the birds flitting through the trees and brush.

I sighed as I rounded the bend to our house.

It is a beautiful house. I thought as it came into sight. It's a shame that I'm not happy here.

Perhaps it was me, and I simply needed more time to adjust to this life. Maybe I wasn't opening myself up and accepting the changes. Being married and moved out to the middle of nowhere was an enormous change. I should give myself grace.

Then, thinking about the pastor's sermon today. I needed to work harder at submitting to my husband, performing my duties, both in and out of the bedroom. Better.

I climbed the few steps to the porch and then turned to look out at our land. We owned this. It was beautiful, with the rolling hills and tall, green trees. Their branches spreading out to create perfectly shaded spots. Perfect for sitting in the hot summer.

"Yes, I would try harder to be accepting of this new life."

Chapter Twelve: Lindsey (May Present Day)

All night, I tossed and turned as I listened for any sound, but nothing came. I hoped that whatever happened yesterday was a fluke. Though it didn't feel like one. That fog or cloud had felt so real. It squeezed and choked me.

I dressed in a t-shirt, jeans, and slip-on tennis shoes. Pulled my hair into a ponytail, then headed into town. As I looked at myself in the full-length mirror, I smiled. This beat my previous wardrobe of dress pants and button-down blouses, and I loved that I didn't need heels any longer.

The encounters with this spirit, or whatever it was, left me shaking a bit. A person could be dealt with, but how do you get rid of a spirit? I'd have to research cleansing with sage. That was a thing, I think? Or maybe a psychic could come to talk to the ghost?

The only thing I knew for sure was this Anna-Rose had lived in this house and this spirit was looking for her. After seeing those pictures at the library, I knew why he had gone after me. I shuttered again, remembering how the cloud had felt.

Today, my plan was breakfast at the diner, followed by a trip to the General Store for batteries and light bulbs. If time permitted, I was going to find out if there was an animal shelter or rescue nearby. I really needed a second set of ears around here.

I pulled into a spot in front of the Wagon Wheel. The sleepy town was quiet and peaceful. I smiled as I stepped out, breathing in the clear air.

The bell on the door chimed as I entered the nearly empty diner.

"Good mornin', hun, sit anywhere." Greeted the ever-present June.

She was the owner and the breakfast waitress for the Wagon Wheel Diner. As with most of the businesses in town, it was family owned and ran by them. Both her daughter, Lara and son, Bart, worked here. June and Lara split the serving duties, and Bart was the afternoon and evening cook. They had a few other townspeople who worked with them to round out the staff.

"Good morning, June."

I scanned the diner as I decided where to sit. Spying an empty booth by the window facing Main Street, I smiled at the few patrons as I made my way to it.

I recognized one as the mailman and another as the owner of the General Store. It didn't open for another hour, so this must be his downtime before starting his workday.

"Coffee?" June asked, pot at the ready.

I could smell the bitter brew as she stood with the pot at the ready. I knew it was Jack's Beans' house blend. June was Jack's grandmother, so it made sense to keep it all in the family.

"Yes, please." I eagerly pushed my mug toward her. "And I'll have the country breakfast. Scrambled eggs. Wheat toast."

"Alrighty. Comin' right up." She said as she finished pouring coffee into the mug.

As she turned to put in my order, I offered a smile of thanks. I then grabbed a sweetener from the dish and poured it in, following it with a splash of the half-and-half June had set on the table. I stirred it absently as I looked out the picture window.

Wisteria was just coming to life. The sun was peeking through the trees, dew was glistening on the bushes and flowers, birds were flitting around. The shop owners were flipping over their closed signs to announce they were open. A school bus rattled around the square as it headed out to the residential area to gather the children for another day of school.

This is just the type of place I needed. It felt good. I took a deep, cleansing breath.

I pulled out my phone and searched the area of animal shelters or rescue groups. I wanted to get an older dog. The closest shelter looked to be two hours away.

I sighed, just as June came with my breakfast.

"Are you looking for a pet, hun?"

"Yeah, a dog. Is there an animal shelter closer than two hours away?"

"Actually, Bart has a litter of mutts he's trying to find homes for. The mama was dumped, and he has been caring for them all."

A puppy. I wasn't sure if I wanted to go through the chewy, potty training, and obedience that was required, but it was an idea.

"Yeah, I *might* be interested. Just the puppies?"

"Nay, he is always takin' in strays. His place is a known spot for dumpin' unwanted animals. He's the local rescue." She chuckled. "Unofficially, of course."

"Oh." That was good to know.

"Yeah, but these pups he has will be great dogs. I'll call him and see if he can meet you before he starts his shift."

As June left, I smiled and started eating my breakfast. I don't know how they cooked their eggs here, but they were the fluffiest I had ever eaten. I was normally an over easy egg girl, but these scrambled eggs had me converting.

As I ate, I reviewed the list of things I needed at the store. More trash bags, batteries, and light bulbs, of course, and I was going to get another flashlight, too. I would not be caught again without one. I was also going to replace all the smoke detects in the house.

One for each bedroom, so five. Plus, kitchen and I wanted an extra in the living room, just in case. Not that I'd ever had a house fire or anything, but it was one of those irrational fears.

June came back over with more coffee.

"Bart said he would bring the puppies up here in a few minutes."

"Oh, now?" It made sense as she had said before his shift, but I thought I could get my errands run first.

"Yes, you *said* you wanted a dog, right?" Her firm tone had me picturing her as a school principal.

My middle-school principal, actually. Mrs. Bird was a sweet lady but had a stern attitude when it came to managing the school and children. My impression of June was much the same.

"Um, yes, of course. Thank you."

She smiled and turned to refill the other diner's coffee mugs.

So, this was happening. I might get a dog today. I had to add things on to the list for that. Dog bowls, a bed, toys, dog food, collar and a leash.

As Bart pulled up with the dogs, I finished up my breakfast. I'd only met him a few times around the diner when I'd come in for meals. I hadn't had much of a personal conversation with him.

"Hey, Lindsey. I got the dogs out back."

"Great." I settled my bill and followed him through the kitchen out the back door.

I heard them before I could see them. They were barking and whining from inside an extra-large kennel in the back of his truck. He opened the tailgate so I could see them more easily. They were fluffy little balls of golden brown and black fur. Tails were wagging and little pink tongues tried to reach me.

"Alrighty, so I got five boys and four girls here. None of them have homes yet, but they're nearly 9 weeks old. Plenty old enough to leave their mama. You'll be gettin' first pick."

"What are they a mix of?"

"A little of this and a little of that." He chuckled. "I'm honestly not sure. Mom looks like she is maybe a German Shepard Mix but really hard to say because she was so small, malnutrition when I got her. She is doing better now."

"That's good. Are you keeping her?"

The puppies licked and chewed on me as I wiggled my fingers between the bars of the kennel. I forgot how sharp puppy teeth were.

"I hadn't thought about it yet." He rubbed his chin. "Do you want her instead of a puppy?"

He whipped out his phone and pulled up a few pictures.

"She's beautiful. Did you name her?" If he named her, he probably wanted to keep her.

"Misty." He looked at her picture. "I don't know why, it just seemed to fit."

My heart sunk a bit. I looked at the puppies. They sure were cute, but I had to be honest with myself. Even though I had time, sort of, I didn't want to deal with all the new puppy things.

Plus, I wasn't sure how things would be once I had guests. Would I be busier seeing to their needs? Plus, I had yet to get my farm animals, so I'm sure they would take a lot of my time.

"To be honest, I was hoping for an older dog, but these guys sure are cute." I wiggled my fingers through the bars again.

"Well, I'm willing to part with her. I already have three others myself and then these little squirts. Plus, these will not be the last rescues of the year. I'm always gettin' new ones." He shook his head. "Sad really."

As I thought about what he said, I nodded, only hesitating a moment before answering.

"I'd love to meet her, if you are sure."

"Yeah. I'm sure. Do you have time to come out to my place? I'm just up the road."

"Yeah, I have time."

"Hop in." He closed the tailgate, and we both jumped in his truck.

I barely knew this man, but I knew June, so I felt safe enough. He was older than me by at least twenty or so years. His wife, Heidi, teaches English to the high schoolers. I'd met her once at the diner. They had four children. Jack was their oldest, who owned Jack's Beans Coffee shop. Then their three daughters had married and moved away.

"So, what made you wake up today and think you needed a dog?"

"Oh, just living out in that house by myself. I thought it would be nice to have an extra set of ears. You know, just in case." I chuckled and looked at him for his reaction. "That probably sounds crazy, right?"

"Not at all. I think you're brave there by yourself." He paused. "I've heard some stories about that old house."

"What kind of stories?"

"People say it's haunted by the ghost of the first owner, James Collins."

"Really?" Though I knew that, I acted surprised.

"Yep, that's why it's been vacant for so long. People say his wife, Anna-Rose, killed him and that's why he haunts the house. Always looking for her."

Despite the Texas heat, I had goosebumps rise all over my body. I wasn't sure that I believed in ghosts, but I knew what I'd experienced. I was going to have to look into the sage thing or something. I could not run a business with that angry spirit running around.

"Do you believe it?" I asked him.

"Honestly, I don't know, but as a teen, we would all sneak over there. There were always weird sounds. Probably just us kids scaring each other. You know how that is?"

I laughed. "Yeah, teens can do silly things."

He pulled down his driveway and the sound of dogs barking grew. I saw Misty immediately. She was a gorgeous golden color dog with flecks of black and darker brown throughout her coat. She was probably about 40 or 50 pounds. Her tail was wagging non-stop.

"That's her there." He pointed to the dog, gestured for me to go to her, while he turned to unload the puppies.

I walked toward her, and she got even more excited, immediately coming to me. It felt like we had an instant connection.

"Hey, girl. Hi, Misty." I pet her as I crouched down to her level. She licked my face and tried to climb into my lap. I scratched her belly and fell in love with her. "And you're sure you want to give her up?"

"Well, honestly, I wasn't until I saw her light up like that. She was clearly meant to be yours." He smiled, setting the last of the puppies behind a gated area. "They're all weaned now, so if you want to take her today, you definitely can. She'll make a good watchdog. She's very alert."

I looked down at her dark eyes and knew she was coming home with me.

"I'm sold. How much do you want for her?"

"Nothing. I know you're good people."

"But you've had vet expenses, food, puppy care. I have to give you something?"

"Nope. She's clearly meant for you, so please. Consider it a welcome to Wisteria gift from one business owner to another."

"Well, okay. Thank you."

He gave me the details of her care, what food she had been eating, and the latest printout from the veterinary showing when she had shots last.

"Dr. Cleary is the best. She'll be happy to hear that Misty has found a good home."

"I do think I'm a good home." I smiled down at her. "I'm sorry you had to bring the puppies into town before."

"Nay, it's good. I know it was probably mom not listening and pushing. That's just how she is."

"She's a sweet lady."

He smiled. "She is."

I thanked him and then realized I didn't have my car here since I rode with him. He must have realized it at the same time I did.

"I'll give you a ride. Just give me two minutes and I'll be ready."

He ran into the house, and a few minutes later, as promised, we were on our way back to town. We talked about dogs and the upcoming Summer Festival on the ride back.

"It is a whole town affair. We'll have a parade and a town wide picnic."

"It sounds fun."

When he pulled up at the back of the Wagon Wheel Diner, I thanked him and then grabbed Misty's leash that he had for her, saving me from having to buy one. Together, Misty and I went to do my errands.

Being a small-town, Bart had let me know she was welcome into the General store. She got a lot of attention and wasn't afraid of anything or anyone. In fact, she seemed to love it, though she looked up at me often. I don't know if it was reassurance she wanted, but I was here for her.

Once my shopping was done, I dropped the bags off at my car and headed over to the veterinary's office as Bart suggested, to get her records transferred to me.

"Hello. Welcome to Wisteria Veterinary Clinic." The receptionist greeted. "Oh, you must be Lindsey. Bart just called, letting us know you had adopted sweet Misty from him." She smiled down at the dog.

"Yes, he said I should stop by and make sure that everything is transferred to me."

"Not a problem. I already started. Here are the forms. If you can complete them, I will finish getting it swapped." She smiled. "Oh, I'm Janet, by the way."

"Nice to meet you, Janet."

I took the forms and sat in the waiting area. Misty followed and sat.

"How did I get so lucky?" I said, petting the dog's head.

She wagged her tail in reply, then laid her head on my leg. I smiled, then got to the business of completing the forms. I gave them a once over before returning them to Janet at the desk.

"All done?"

"Yes." I handed them over.

"Great. Just give me a minute." Janet said. She began typing into the computer. "Alright, there you go. She won't be due for shots until... looks like March."

"Perfect." That gave me nearly a year before she would need anything.

"Do you have any questions for me or the doctor? I can get her."

"Um, no, I think we'll be good. I've had a dog before and she seems well-behaved."

"She's a good one for sure. It's a shame someone just dumped her."

"Yes, so sad. She's such a sweet dog."

I looked down at the sweet dog's face. I was already in love with the brown-eyed beauty. Who could have dumped such a beautiful dog? I'd only known her for a little over an hour, but I already couldn't imagine being without her.

After thanking Janet, my errands in town were done. I got Misty back to my car. She hopped right in without a fuss.

"Let's go home, girl."

She wagged her tail.

Chapter Thirteen: Lindsey (May Present Day)

The first night with Misty was a bit rough. After everything seemed to go so smoothly during the day, once it was time to settle down for bed, she began whining and pacing.

"What's wrong, girl?"

She came to me, climbing into my lap. I scratched her all over.

"Do you miss your babies?"

She wagged her tail. I know Bart said they were weaned. That didn't mean she wouldn't miss them.

"I'm sure they will be fine."

I spread out a soft blanket for her. She smelled it, did a few circles, scratched at it a little, then laid down.

"Better?"

She wagged her tail and only whimpered a little. We both slept fairly well, and except for a few creaks, there were no ghostly disturbances.

The next day, I woke more rested than I had in years. Misty looked up at me with a puppy smile.

"Did you sleep well, Misty?"

She yipped and wagged her tail. We both stretched, and then I let her outside, leaving the door open so she could come in when she was ready. While I waited, I started some coffee, then I added a scoop of food to her bowl and freshened her water.

I sat on one of the left behind rickety chairs. My new kitchen table would be delivered soon, and I couldn't wait. It would sure be better than this old set. I swore at any moment this one was going to fall apart.

I enjoyed the view from here as I could see my garden. It was still baby plants and new sprouts, but I was proud of my work. Next up, I was going to add a few farm animals. Chickens, a pig or two, and some goats seemed like a good start. Maybe even a couple of donkeys. There were a lot of options.

I had little experience, but how hard could it be? I laughed at myself. I knew it would not be easy, but I had confidence that I could do it. Spending those few years helping on my aunt and uncle's farm had given me a good foundation. I'd loved it. I'd gotten to do a little of everything.

The floorboard creaked. I froze. My pulse quickened as I listened as the sound moved from upstairs to downstairs. The heavy stomp of footsteps moved toward me.

That's when Misty burst in with a quick bark and a wag of her tail. She went straight to her food bowl. She took a mouth full, eating it up, then looked at me with a thankful smile and a wag of her tail.

The creaking stopped and could have sworn I heard a curse in the air. Maybe getting the dog was the right thing to deal with this spirit. I gave myself a mental high-five.

"Good girl." As I stood to get another cup of coffee, I rubbed her head.

I dropped a couple of pieces of toast into the toaster and then slathered it with strawberry jam once it popped up. At the farmer's market, a local farmer sold various jams and jellies.

I took both the fresh coffee and toast on the back porch. Misty followed me and explored the yard.

This was hands down my favorite spot to sit and enjoy the morning. The beautiful view of the rolling hills, stretching trees, and orange-pink sunrise.

The caw of crows caught my attention. I looked up at one of the big trees to find it full of large, black crows.

"That can't be good."

They sat in the trees, staring out, bouncing up and down, and cawing at each other. Or maybe it was me. A shiver ran through me as they suddenly took flight, leaving in a black cloud.

Yikes.

Shaking the creepy feeling, I cleared my breakfast dishes and then went to get ready for the day.

I had an appointment with the records department in town. I wanted to get more information on the house, even though all my remodeling was done. Given the disturbances I was experiencing, it was another step in learning more about what I'd gotten myself into.

I had continued to read Anna-Rose's journals. It was interesting to read, in her words, her adventure and life. I could almost picture the house back then.

She described it as basically two rooms. The combination kitchen and living area, then there was the bedroom. It was the one I was using now, though I have a feeling it has changed a bit since her days here.

Once I was ready, I told the dog goodbye, securing her inside the house. She yawned and settled on her blanket. I hoped she would be okay while I was gone.

Hopefully she slept the whole time, but I'd try to be quick just in case. And, while I'd been able to take her into the General Store yesterday, I didn't think city hall was an appropriate place for a dog.

As I drove down Main Street on my way to city hall, I realized I hadn't paid much attention to it yet. When I parked in the lot of the two story brick building, I realized why.

It was an unassuming building set back from the street, causing to not really stand out. The landscaping around it was clean and neat, and the structure itself looked well kept, like much of the town. The residents took a lot of pride in their home.

I stepped inside and was not surprised that it was also unpretentiously adorned. The lobby area was a gray travertine tile. There was no reception or information desk. The stairs were directly in front and then there were offices with simple black and white name plate to either side of me.

"Tax office. Water department." I mumbled, reading them off.

Then I saw the sign pointing to the records down the hall. I followed it until I reached a closed door. Unsure if I should knock or just go in, I decided to try the handle. It was unlocked, so I opened it.

A dark-haired lady looked up from a desk with a smile. "Hi, welcome. Are you Lindsey?"

"Hi, yes, I am. Sorry I wasn't sure if I should knock or—"

"This is Texas. We just walk on in." She stood and came over to greet me with a firm handshake. "I'm Dottie. It's nice to meet the new owner of the Collins' place. I never thought we would get it sold again."

"That doesn't sound good."

"Oh, it's a beautiful property, but the stories about the ghost keep it empty." She snickered. "I've never witnessed it myself, but even the mayor swears she's had an encounter with it."

"Really?"

This was becoming my standard reaction. People all had a story, and I pretended it was my first time hearing about the house.

"Oh yeah. Mostly just bumps and thumps around the house. Not much else, but some people, a few, said they heard a voice calling for Anna-Rose. That was the wife who first lived there."

Chills ran through my body. "I've heard that too."

"The stories or the voice?"

"Both."

"Wow, so it's true?"

"I guess so."

I didn't mention that I had an intense encounter with the ghost. I can't even explain what happened to me that day. It was almost like he was choking me, or at least holding me firmly in place. Since I was still processing it, I wasn't ready to tell anyone else about it.

"Well, let's get you that information you were looking for. I already got most of it pulled out for you. I have it all set up in the next room for you."

She gestured for me to follow her. As we stepped through a doorway, she turned on the lights to a large room with rows of file cabinets. To one side was a large conference table with stacks of files and papers on it.

"Here's what I pulled. So, the interesting thing is that everyone calls it the Collins' house, but they actually weren't the first owners. There was a man by the name of Samuel Thomas. He only owned the property for a year or two, before he sold it to the Collins. There is no record of him ever living there, though, and James Collins was the first to build a house on it. It was said that there was only a small shack on it prior to that, but we don't have complete records from that time."

"Oh, interesting."

"Also, the property used to be nearly 600 acres. It was divided up and sold in 1919."

"Oh wow, so she sold it down to the 20 acres it is now?"

"Yes, and it looks like it was around then that she expanded the house a bit. Not to its current state, but she expanded the living room and kitchen. According to this, it was a 700 square foot clapboard house, and she updated the entire house to a 1,300 square foot house in 1920."

"Do you know when the second floor was added?"

"Yes, I found it after we spoke." She flipped through some files. "In 1948, the property was bought and turned into a home for unwed mothers. That's when the house was upgraded to its current state, or well, the two stories. I've heard you have really cleaned it up, though."

"I have. I think it looks good. I still have a bit more to do, but I'm planning to open the bed-and-breakfast in a two weeks."

"That's so exciting." She smiled. "We love new business owners around here."

"Well, I hope I can make the town proud."

"So, what else can I tell you about the property?"

"Do you know how long the unwed mother's home was open? Were they the last residents?"

"Oh, no, they were definitely not the last. It has been a revolving door of residents until... Let's see... 2005. Nobody has lived there since, though the town has tried to keep it at least somewhat maintained."

"Oh-okay." I wasn't sure what I would do with that information, but it was good to know. I wanted to ask more, but the question sounded crazy. Oh, what the heck? "Do you know why nobody stays in this house?"

"The ghost."

"Ah, I should have known." I knew, but still wanted to ask.

"Yes, people say he has scared away many."

"Um, okay. Well, thank you." Still not sure what I would do with this new information, but my stomach felt a little queasy hearing this news.

"Well, if you ever need to look through anything again, you are always welcome here."

"Thank you so much."

I left feeling heavy. I trudged my way to my car. What if this ghost ruined my business, too? I didn't have a back-up plan, and I sure wasn't going back to California. With Derek in it, the state just wasn't big enough.

My phone chimed just as I got to my car. It was Simone.

Call if you have time

I hit her number.

"Hey, girl."

"Hey. What's up?"

"There is no easy way to say this, but I wanted you to hear it from me."

"Uh-oh, are you okay?"

"Yeah, I'm okay, but are you sitting?"

"Not exactly. I was just about to get into my car. I came to city hall to learn more about my house."

"Anything good?"

"Not really. Except for the original owner, well sort of original owner, nobody else has stayed in this house for long. It has been empty since 2005, if you can believe that."

"Why not?"

"Okay, you *are not* going to believe me, but it's haunted."

"Wait, what?"

"Yeah. People think by the husband. They'd been married only two years, when he was killed."

"Wow, that's a crazy story. Do you think it's haunted?"

"Honestly, yes." How much was I going to share? "I've heard a lot of weird things that can't be explained."

"I am never coming to visit you."

I laughed, "Yes, you are, and I'm sure it's nothing. Harmless."

"If you say so." She laughed. "Well, okay, now I don't know if I should tell you this news."

"You can't do that to me. You can't dangle gossip and then pull it back."

"Fine." I heard her exhale. "Derek and his new... um... person are pregnant."

I'm so glad I wasn't driving yet because I would have driven off the road for sure.

"Are you serious?"

"Afraid so. You know Jarred works with Derek's dad. He told him."

"Well... um... I'm glad you told me, and doubly glad that I moved when I did."

"I couldn't have you finding out any other way. You okay?"

"No, honestly, no, but I will be." I could feel the tears coming, but I wouldn't cry until I was at home.

We said goodbye. I climbed into the car before the tears started. I held it in until I saw the house. That's when the tears burst free. I sat in the car staring at it with tears streaming down my face.

"Now I really want this to work. I have to succeed." Ghost be damned, I added in my head.

Chapter Fourteen: Lindsey (May Present Day)

Today I was trading my car in for a truck. It only made sense to do that, as I'd be hauling hay and animal feed soon. It had been a bear to haul lumber to the house, though I'd managed.

Once I had the truck, I was going to buy a livestock trailer. I actually I already had one bought from one of the neighbors, but I couldn't pick it up until I had the truck. He agreed to keep it on his property until I got my truck.

After doing some research, I had settled on a small dealership just outside of Wisteria. They had a variety of trucks, and I should get a nice price for my car. It was only six years old and paid off last year.

It was never wrecked and had all the regular maintenance, well, mostly on time. It had a few dings and nicks from parking lots, but otherwise, it was in good condition.

There were rows of pickup trucks in the lot. A sign indicated visitor parking, so I parked in one of the empty spots. I eyed them all, thinking that one of these was going home with me today, but which one?

"I can't believe I'm doing this." I mumbled to myself and fought a squeal.

"Howdy, there." A man in a tan cowboy hat called out. "My name is Bobby. Can I help you?"

"Oh, hi, yes. I'm Lindsey. I'm looking to trade my car in for a truck."

"Alrighty. What do you have in mind? Will you be towing?"

"Yes, so I have a small farm. I recently purchased a livestock trailer. In researching, I need something heavy duty that can tow about 20,000 pounds. I was thinking the minimum I would want is a half-ton truck, but I'm willing to go a bit bigger. Though it might be a little overkill, I'm thinking investing in a bigger truck now will mean if my needs increase, I won't be stuck later."

"Whoa, you came in prepared." He rubbed his chin as he scanned the lot. "I got a few. Right this way."

I followed him to the front row. I'm sure with the prime spots in the lot, they were going to have a grade A price tag too, but I would hear him out.

"So here you have a few. Now most of these are diesel, so obviously, different from what you put in your car."

I nodded, fighting the urge to roll my eyes. Was he going to start mansplaining to me? When he saw the idea of diesel did not faze me, he cleared his throat and continued to explain features to me before moving into pricing.

"Well, okay, but before I decide, can I see how much I'll get for my car?"

"Yes, sure. Let me get someone looking at it."

I handed him my key.

"Why don't you keep looking around and I'll be right back."

I peeked in the couple of trucks he had pointed out. They were all new, it really came down to features in them. I knew from others in town that air conditioning was a must have, but more than that, I just wanted to ensure when I needed to haul animals or pick up feed, I could do it.

Even before Bobby came back, I had decided on a dark blue Dodge with an extended cab and an extra-long bed. I hadn't driven a truck in something like ten years, so this was going to take some practice. I haven't pulled anything since then either.

My neighbor, Steve, who was selling me the trailer, had offered to let me practice and he would coach me. I think it was his wife, Charlie, who had nudged him to the idea.

I knew I'd need the practice, so I took him up on it.

Ole Bobby came back with a grin. "Did you make a decision?"

"Maybe, but again, I'd like to hear how much for my car first."

"Right. I have one guy running it through the tests now. We should know soon." He looked around. "Um, so do you wanna take one for a test drive, perhaps?"

"Actually, yes, this blue Dodge here."

"Ah, good choice. Let me grab the keys." He jogged back to the office while I stood in the scorching sun.

Why were car dealerships always so hot? There was never shade. If I really thought about it, it was just a giant parking lot, so no reason for shade. I fanned myself as I peeked into the Dodge again.

"Here we are." Bobby came jogging back across the lot, rattling the keys. He handed them to me, and we both climbed in. "You'll need to warm up the engine slightly, but with these newer models, it doesn't need to be more than a few minutes or so."

"Alright." I turned it on and then we sat there while the engine warmed.

He started pointing out the various features. The navigation system and radio were a nice upgrade from my previous one. My sedan was nice, but it had a basic radio.

"And you can download an app which will connect to it... here. See?"

"Nice. Okay."

"Alright, ready to ride."

"Yes, it's been a minute since I've driven a large truck, so this will be a good test." I chuckled nervously. Putting it in reverse, I slowly made my way out of the lot and followed Bobby's direction for my test driving path.

The truck handled smoothly. It was large and heavy, but responsive. If the pricing all worked out between this and my trade-in, this was going to be my new truck.

We finished the test drive and Bobby told me to park in front of the building. We walked in and he showed me to an office.

"Can I get you a water or coffee?"

"Water, thank you."

"Great. I'm going to check on your car while I grab that."

Hours later, after haggling and waiting and haggling, I was driving away with my gorgeous new truck. It was going to take a little getting used to, but it was perfect.

The next day, I headed over to the Marshall's farm to pick up my trailer and to practice hooking it up and driving with it. As I pulled down their driveway, I saw Charlie step out onto the porch and wave.

I had only met her once, the day I came to look at the trailer after seeing an ad for it posted at the General Store. The Marshalls were high school sweethearts, and around my age, with two young children.

She gestured for me to drive on to the barn, so I followed the driveway, then parked in front of my trailer. I hopped out of the truck just as she came around.

"Hello. What a gorgeous truck?"

"Thanks. It should pull this easily."

"Definitely."

Steve came from inside the barn, letting out a whistle as he gave my truck a once-over.

"That's a beaut. Get that from Ole Bobby, didja? He is a bit of an a-hole, am I right?" He chuckled. "Ready for your trailer?"

"I am." Ready to get new animals on the farm, too. I just had a few more things to complete first, but I kept all that to myself.

Steve ran through a few how-tos on the trailer, then we started the hands-on part of the demo. I turned my truck around, backing until he gave me the signal to stop.

"Now, see how far you are away from everything? Look in all your mirrors so you get a good feel for it, because you will likely have to do this by yourself sometimes." I nodded and looked as he told me. "Alrighty, now hop out and let's hook this baby up."

I followed all his directions until I heard everything click, then tugged at it to be sure it was secure.

"Great. Now, pull forward and over to the left there. Watch for me as I'll give you hand signals."

He had me pull this way, back-up, that way, back-up. Then I drove around the barn to the front and back, then reversed again. It was thirty minutes of driving all over his property, parking in different spots, and backing through it.

"I think you've got this down, no problem at all."

"Thanks so much. This is really great of you both to help me with this."

"That's what neighbors are for." Charlie said as she handed me a basket of fresh veggies.

"Wow, thank you. These smell amazing." I smiled, taking the basket. "I hope I can return the favor one day."

They shared a look. "Do you babysit?"

"I do." Not that I have done much since I was a teen, but that sounded fun.

"Well, then we will be in touch." Charlie leaned forward to hug me.

I loaded my vegetables into the cab, waved, and then pulled my new trailer home. It was a little challenging on the narrow roads with other cars on it. The Marshalls farm didn't have moving obstacles, so it had been easy.

I finally pulled down my long driveway and around to the barn. I turned and backed so I could park the trailer on the side of the barn. There was a concrete pad already in place that I naturally assumed was for this purpose.

Things were really coming together for me here. I could not wait to welcome guests.

Chapter Fifteen: Lindsey (June Present Day)

Except for being a little anxious the first night, Misty had settled in with no problem. Now, after living here for a week, she had claimed more than half of my bed for herself.

She only used her blanket during the day. So, at night, I slept in the upper right corner, but I'd never felt safer than having my beautiful mutt here with me.

My ghostly resident had been quiet since bringing Misty home. There had been a few creaks and bumps around, but nothing like before.

I'd been able to get the last two boxes unpacked and the new smoke detectors installed. My new furniture had arrived as well and looked fabulous.

"Now we just need to finish setting up the guest bedrooms." I told the dog as she followed me around. "It will be nice to have people in the house, right?"

She simply wagged her tail.

"I'll take that as a yes." I scratched her ears.

Since the new beds had arrived, I'd purchased all the linens, pillows, and all new towels. It was simply a matter of making beds and adding decorative pieces to each room.

I wanted that down home feeling. Vases with flowers, farm landscape artwork, and soft curtains that matched the bedding were all ready to be set out.

I went into the first bedroom. This one had a queen-sized bed in it. I grabbed the fitted sheet and snapped it out as I started making the beds. As I smoothed it flat, I smiled. These sheets were soft and smooth, especially after I washed them for the first time.

"My guests are going to be so lucky."

I finished making the bed. Then I started hanging artwork, laying out the decoration items on the dresser and on a rustic shelf I had found among the left behind furniture.

Then, for the final touch, I added the curtains. They were layered with one gauzy one and then thicker blackout curtains over those. But these didn't look like heavy curtains. They were soft, with a beautiful pastel floral print.

I stepped back when I was done, sighing as my dream was turning to reality. It was exactly how I pictured it would look. It had a homelike feel, but with a luxury of being a way. I peeked in the closest, spreading out the dozen clothes hangers.

Then I moved to the doorway.

"Ready for the first guests?"

I repeated the process in the other three rooms, then both bathrooms got sacks of fluffy towels and fresh smelling soaps. I cleaned the mirrors until they shined.

"Awesome."

Next up was to tackle the attic, but first a lunch break. Anything to put that room off, but I needed to get it done.

I took my salad out on the back porch. Misty followed and ran out into the yard to smell around.

I kicked back and took in the view. At noon, the view was both the same and different. The sun was high in the air, so the trees filtered the light, creating dappled shade. It would be perfect for families to picnic under or children to run around.

I had set up an area to play horseshoes and cornhole. Adding benches for hanging out.

"Just a little more work and I'd be ready."

I finished my lunch and headed in so I could tackle the last house project and the one I was most dreading.

As I made my way upstairs, I peeked in one bedroom, taking in my work from earlier. I squealed a bit as I continued my trek toward the attic. I had my two flashlights, the light bulbs, gloves, and a couple of heavy-duty contractor bags. I headed up cautiously.

As I stepped into the room, I took a deep breath.

I can do this. I thought.

I looked down at my sidekick. At least with her here, I felt safer. She got right to work investigating the new to her space.

I got the lone light bulb changed, then turned on the light.

"Ta-da!"

This was my first good look at the entire attic. It was larger than I'd realized, and there was a lot more stuff up here than I thought as well. Boxes and trunks were tucked in all the eves and along all the walls. This was going to take some time.

"Might as well get started."

Overwhelmed by the amount of stuff, I turned around and around as I tried to decide which pile to dive into.

"I guess with that pile over there." I sighed and marched to the farthest corner.

It looked like the roof leak had damaged most of this. I slipped on the gloves and snapped open the first bag.

The first couple of boxes were completely ruined. I saved what I could out of them, but most of the contents went into the bag. It appeared to be a lot of old papers. There were a few items that I could read giving hints it was from the unwed mothers time frame for the house.

The next one had kitchen items in it. Old plates, bowls, and glasses with beautiful floral patterns on them. They were all in good condition, considering their age.

These would be fun to use with guests. I set them into one of the undamaged boxes, then moved on. An hour later, I'd filled the bags and carried them to the trash cans outside, grabbing more bags as I headed back-up.

"Giving up on me, girl?" I said as I stepped over Misty, sleeping at the bottom of the stairs. I guess she'd tired of following me all over and could monitor me from there.

Diving back in, I assessed what I'd gotten done so far.

"Only a little more to go."

I had a stack of stuff to keep and possibly use in my bed-and-breakfast, such as the dishes I'd found earlier. Then there was a whole pile of things I had no idea what to do with yet.

It was clothing and linens that looked to be from Anna-Rose and James. They were amazing, but I didn't know what to do with those. Could I donate them to a charity or maybe give them to Brenda for the town museum?

A day after I'd gotten the journals from Brenda, I had grabbed an ice cream with Molly at Sprinkles and Cream. I loved their special, which was called Sprinkles and Cream. It was a mix of vanilla ice cream with fun sprinkles, just as the name implies. I also got it in one of their handmade cones.

Molly and I had become quick friends, so I loved to meet up with her about one a week, either for coffee, a cone, or a blue-plate special at the Wagon Wheel.

Over the ice cream, we were discussing Anna-Rose and her journals.

"So now you know a bit more about your house and Anna-Rose."

"Yes, interesting story." I licked at a sweet drip that was trying to make its way down my hand. "The journals give me a better picture of her life. She seemed so sad."

"Yeah, she had a sad, alone life, at least in part. I think she had a lot of friends in town and was an active member of the committee. Many of the festivals we have today are because she had originally organized them."

"Wow, that's amazing."

"I was sad to hear that she never remarried and never had children."

"Yeah, that's sad for sure." I said, but then I was already 39. I wasn't married any longer, and I didn't have children. Could I turn into Anna-Rose? Was I her?

Thinking about it now, I still felt sad for her. She had only been married for two years. Whatever happened to him, she never found love again. I wanted to know more about her. Perhaps when I got to that part in her journals, it would give me a glimpse of the why.

I finished the attic, bringing the last of the trash down and then the items I planned to use. For now, I would leave the old clothes and various household items that I wouldn't use packed upstairs, but overall, the attic was cleaned up.

I got a glass of water, then decided to read a few pages in her journals. I started again with the first one because it was my favorite. She was full of hope and love. It was happy and joyful, and in so many ways, reminded me of my own journey.

She traveled from Virginia to Texas, which blew my mind that she was also originally from Richmond, Virginia. That is where I was born and raised. I moved away when I left for college and then met Derek, so I married him and moved to California.

It's weird that we had such similar backgrounds.

"And we look alike." I eyed the picture that Brenda had tucked in the journal.

An hour in, I was more than the few pages in that I'd planned to read, but I could help it. Her life paralleled mine is so many ways.

Finally, I got to the sad and depressing parts. When I read the first time he hit her, I nearly jumped out of the chair. She was clearly heartbroken by this, as would I.

"What changed, James?" I said to the house.

I kept reading until it got dark out. There were pages and pages of her sadness and his anger. It really tore at my heart. The words seemed so familiar, which was strange. Just like the feeling I had when I first stepped into the house, I knew before flipping the page what was coming next.

I put them away carefully and started my dinner. Her words haunted me. I could almost feel her pain through the journal.

"I hope you are getting to rest now, Anna-Rose."

Chapter Sixteen: Anna-Rose (1882)

James had been home from Fort Worth for a week now. He came home angrier and meaner than usual. He hadn't gotten a good deal on the cattle, and then lost several on the way home with them. He had hired one cowboy to help me drive them.

I didn't voice my thoughts, but trying to wrangle 300 head of cattle with just two people was doomed from the start. He wouldn't have listened to me about it. I was a woman, and he knew better than me, or at least that's been his attitude when I have made suggests.

If he would listen, I would have suggested he hire ranch hands. He said help was too expensive, and we needed every dime to make this ranch work.

I was only good enough to do the cleaning and cooking, caring for the farm animals, but not cattle. I wasn't smart enough for that. Just the things like whitewashing the walls, beating the rugs, restuffing the mattress each fall. Woman's work.

I laughed privately at this ignorance.

Despite his foul mood, I had news that I couldn't wait to share with him, but he took it poorly and not at all how I thought he would. This was the first of many beatings.

"I have too much stress to deal with a child! You should have controlled this better." He grabbed me by the throat, then began hitting me over and over while screaming at me. "Children are selfish and take and take. We do not need that right now!"

How was I supposed to control this? I knew that there were some products or methods, most illegal, but I wanted children. We were married, and that's what most married people did.

"I did nothing wrong." I cried as I desperately tried to protect my stomach.

The hits came over and over, and it seemed that my cries and struggles fueled his anger. He shook me, punched me, throwing me down once he was done.

He leaned over me for a moment before yelling into my face. "Don't let my dinner be late!"

Then he stomped out of the house.

I laid on the floor, wallowing in the abuse and sadness. My body hurt, every part of me ached from his fists and hurtful words.

"Please be okay, little one. Please." I whispered. I touched my stomach gingerly, flinching at the pain.

I couldn't stay here any longer, so before he caught me lying around, I pushed myself up, wincing at the ache throbbing through my body. I went to the sink to wash my face. Then I began cooking supper for my abuser.

The next day, Saturday, I caught my reflection. I was bruised head to toe. How was I going to go to church tomorrow looking like this? What would people think?

I frowned as I thought that based on the recent sermons, they would probably think I wasn't doing my duties. I would just not go until the bruising went away.

I put my hand softly over my belly.

"Okay, little one, please stay safe." I murmured. It had been my plea that I had said all night.

"Who the hell are you talking to?" James said, startling me.

"Myself." I braced myself for his fist, but it didn't come. Thank goodness.

"Idiot." He muttered as he walked out of the house.

The name-calling I could deal with. I sighed in relief, then busied myself working on the meals for the day, which would include baking bread for the week.

Halfway through, I got dizzy and had to sit for a moment with a glass of water. I kept an eye out in case James came in, but thankfully I could see he was out in the far pasture.

After several minutes, I felt a bit better. I sighed, pushing myself up. A wash of dizziness came over me again. I swayed as everything went black. When I came to, James was standing over me.

"What happened?" My voice hoarse.

"I don't know. I came in and you were on the floor." He said flatly.

That's when I felt it. Wetness between my legs. I looked down to see blood staining my dress and pooled on the ground.

"The baby." I cried.

He picked me up, whispering softly to me as he carried me to the bedroom. He laid me gently on the bed, then went out to the kitchen. I could hear water sloshing and the slight squeak of the water pump. I laid in bed in shock.

I lost my baby. Tears stung my eyes.

He came back with a bowl of water. He wiped my face, then took my clothes off. I tried to fight him, but he continued.

"Let me get you changed. Be still." He whispered.

When I realized he was trying to help; I let him. He got me into clean bed clothing, then brought me a glass of water and put a cool rag on my forehead.

"Rest now, Anna-Rose."

I laid there awake, processing what had happened. The hot tears flowed. I had lost the baby. That thought kept replaying in my mind.

He had caused me to lose it. He made this happen. The pain in my body was not nearly as bad as the ache in my heart. I felt betrayed.

At some point, I fell asleep, sleeping off and on for a few hours. The last time I woke, it was dark outside, and James was not in the bed.

I needed to use the outhouse, so I got out of bed and made my way down the hall and into the combination kitchen and living room. That's when I noticed him bundled up, laying on a blanket on the floor near the fire.

I didn't disturb him as I grabbed the rifle and the oil lamp, then made my way carefully to the outhouse. I hated this part of living here. Back home, we had indoor plumbing, but considering the closest people were over 5 miles away, I knew I was safe from prying eyes.

It was the wolves, bears, and other wildlife that I had to worry about out here.

Once I was back in the house, I put the rifle and oil lamp away, got more water, and headed back to bed.

Through all of that, I did not wake James. I was relieved because, while he had been sweet to allow me to rest, he could be anger as a wet cat, with little reason. No, it was best to let him be for the night.

The next day, I woke with tears in my eyes. I knew it yesterday, but upon waking, I fully realized what had happened. I was trying to process all that happened.

The baby was gone. He had beaten it out of me. Perhaps it was the guilt of that causing him to take care of me last night. All I knew at that moment was the baby was gone and I needed to do better to not make him angry.

I went out to fetch eggs and milk, then I started the coffee on the stove and began cooking breakfast. I had thick slices of ham, eggs, and biscuits with strawberry preserves.

"Good morning. How're you feeling?" He asked, coming from our bedroom.

He had dressed for the day, so he must have woke while I was out doing my chores.

"Hollow, but better." I smiled. "Thank you for taking care of me."

"You are my wife." He said flatly.

I wanted to laugh at that, as he hadn't shown he cared much about me until now. He hadn't even flinched at my hollow comment. I meant it as an insult to him. He let it roll.

He got a tin mug and filled it with coffee, then took his seat at the table. I laid the plate of food in front of him. He grunted a thank you and then got down to the business of eating. Not another word to me. Not an apology or concern for my health.

Watching him turned my stomach. There was no hint of guilt at killing our baby. He could simply go on living normally while the baby was gone. He killed it, but his life didn't look impact. While I was heartbroken and betrayed. I fought the urge to scream.

Once he had his fill, he went to do his chores. I cleaned up and then went out to kill a chicken for our dinner and supper. I had some canned vegetables that I could serve with it, along with some fresh ones from the garden.

With the chicken cleaned and butchered, I got it seasoned and started frying it. A few hours later, our meal was prepared, and I heard James coming back. He stopped at the outside water pump and then he stomped in.

He plodded in his chair and then looked up at me.

"Isn't it Sunday?"

"Yes."

"You didn't go to church."

"No." I didn't explain that between the bruising and miscarriage, I was not up for it this one week. Instead, I had read the bible alone while the food cooked. My private sermon, if you will.

He shrugged and then looked for his plate. I set it in front of him with a forced smile. He mumbled something that I couldn't understand and, frankly, I could not care less what he had to say right now. I hope he choked on his food.

My appetite was almost non-existent, but I tried. I had eaten little at breakfast as well, but I no longer had to feed a baby, so it didn't matter. Nothing mattered, except not upsetting James.

James finished and grunted for more. I served him without words. He ate, muttered something, and then left.

It was like this for a few weeks with almost no words said between, but he also hadn't hit me, nor did he try to have sex with me. I wasn't going to complain to either. It was a pleasant break that I knew wouldn't last.

Chapter Seventeen: Lindsey (June Present Day)

I walked around the stalls at one of my neighboring farm, the Jenkins Family Farm. They had baby goats, chickens, and even a few pigs for sale.

I had everything else in the house ready. My first guests would arrive in one week, so this was the last step to my agritourism bed-and-breakfast. It was exciting.

I hadn't given myself as much time as I should to get acclimated to caring for all the baby animals before guests would start arriving. It was okay, though. I would try to keep it manageable and add more as I became more comfortable with the various chores.

After cleaning out the attic, I spent the next day preparing my barn and yard to get my farm animals. I had finally gotten the chicken coop and barn ready just yesterday, which included a quick trip to the feed store. Where I'd gotten stocked on all the necessary supplies to feed and care for my future pets. Even though I didn't know exactly what I would get, I had a general idea, so I bought feed for that type of animal.

Even though I had some limited experience, I'd done a ton of research online, but going into the feed store gave me an opportunity to ask questions. It also gave me a chance to ask about who and where to get my new animals from.

"Sorry to ease drop." A woman in jeans, t-shirt, and a bright smile said. "I'm Marley Jenkins. I'm up the road from you, Jenkins Family Farm. We have a bunch of baby goats right now. I have a million baby chicks and a few piglets left. We sometimes have other animals available, just not currently. You're welcome to stop by anytime."

"Oh, thank you."

It didn't surprise me she knew who I was. I was becoming used to that. It was a small-town, and I was the newest resident.

We exchanged information and set a date for me to come look at them, which was today.

"They are all so cute. How am I supposed to pick?" I giggled at the sweet faces. Then reached forward to scratch a tri-colored goat that stuck its head forward.

"Do you want to go in with them? Then maybe they'll speak to you." Marley gestured towards the gate.

"You have a beautiful farm." I said as I walked in with the goats.

"Oh, thanks." Her bright smile shone with pride in ownership.

"I'd love to learn more from you."

"I'd be happy to answer any questions or help you."

The baby goats swarmed me, and I squatted down to greet them.

"So, these two are pygmy goats. That white one with the brown face is a boar goat. They are great in the Texas heat. I actually have two more running around here... oh, over there napping."

"They're all so cute. I was thinking I'd start with four or five and does to start out with. No bucks, yet." I had learned the terms for females and males. I'd wanted to sound like I knew what I was doing.

"That's a good plan. When you are ready to breed, we can loan one of our non-related bucks or the Washingtons up the road have good males as well."

I made a mental note.

"How many does do you have?"

"Ten currently for sale, and then eight bucks. I have two mamas about to kid. I'm on birthing watch 24/7 right now."

"Oh, wow. Do you have to help them?"

"Sometimes, but most of mine are experienced moms. These two here," she picked up two tiny black, gray, and white babies, "were born to my least experienced mom and they are doing great. Both girls. I would definitely recommend these two. They're weaned and ready."

"I like the idea of sisters." I rubbed their heads. "Okay. Two so far."

I looked around and pointed to a brown and white one. She nodded. I had to keep checking for which ones were boys versus girls before I fell in love with anymore.

"How about this almost black one and that tri-colored one?" I had already fallen in love with the tri-colored through the fence, so it just made sense to take her home with me.

"Perfect. I think these are all good picks."

We got them loaded into my trailer where I'd already added a bed of hay for them and there was feed and water in troughs as well.

Next, we went to pick out chickens. We went to a different part of her barn where she had chicks in incubators.

"Okay, these here are all ready to go. What I recommend for first timers are these here. This one is a barred Plymouth Rock. They will be a spotty, brown color when grown. Their pattern makes it hard for predators to spot them. They have a good temperament and produce a lot of eggs each year."

I nodded, making mental notes as she spoke. I had already done some Google searches for chicken breeds, and this was one I was leaning towards.

"These here are Orpingtons. They are sweet things. They come in a few colors, most of mine are the buff color. Think golden-brown. Really pretty. They get along well with most of the other breeds. Then finally we have the most common which is the Rhode Island Red or RIRs. They can be a bit ornery, but they seem to do okay with these other two breeds for some reason. All of these will give you a ton of eggs."

"How many do you recommend I start with?"

"Depends on how much room you have, but as I know the Collins place a bit, I'd say you could get away with at least a dozen to start with, and then you can add to that as you get more comfortable. You can get a mix of chicks, too." She paused. "I know I said a dozen, but if you're prepared, you could get four to six of each of these three types. What do you think?"

I looked at the little babies peeping and chirping. They were all so cute. I definitely had planned for a whole, huge flock, but that would come with time, or maybe today.

"Okay, I'll take six of each."

"Great! I'll grab a box." She left and came back with a sturdy cardboard box with a layer of hay in the bottom.

We picked through the babies, selecting the cutest, in my opinion, ones of the flock. They peeped as we got them gathered up.

"I'll leave them here in the warmth while we look at the piglets."

I nodded and followed her to the next room. I could hear and smell them long before I saw them. The smell took me right back to my summers on my aunt and uncle's farm. Pigs had always been my favorite.

They kept them for meat, so they always warned me not to get too attached because, come Fall, they would be on our plates. It didn't matter. Each year I'd name them, but I never cried at Thanksgiving when they would bring out the big ham. I understood.

With that said, I didn't plan to raise mine for meat. I would get that from the store or one of my wonderful neighbors.

"So, do you have a pig pen ready? They need a sturdy fence."

"Yes, I remember from my limited time helping my aunt and uncle. They always used hardwood posts and extra supports."

"Perfect." She smiled. "I have two breeds here. This is the Red Wattle. They are fairly docile, but can startle easily, so be sure you don't sneak up on them."

"I'll be sure to make a lot of noise." I said, laughing.

"Ha, yes, do that. Then I have these." She pointed to the pen next to it. "These are Yorkshire pigs or Large White Pigs as they are sometimes called. This is a good one to start with too, I think. It's the most common pig in the U.S., so you can find a ton of information on it and people easily recognize it too."

I studied both for a moment.

"Do you have two red wattles that are females?"

"I do." She clapped her hands together softly and climb in with the little piggies.

She started pointing and holding up piglets. I selected the two quietest ones, not that any of them were quiet. Lucky for me that I loved the pig's squealing sound.

"Good choices."

She handed them over the fence to me and then climbed out. Once out, she took the second one, and we headed for my truck. We put the two pigs in a separate compartment from the goats, then went back to get the chickens. I loaded those into another compartment.

"You got a good trailer. You get it from Steve and Charlie?"

"Thanks. Yeah, nice people."

"They are. Definitely good ones to know. They don't have much livestock anymore as they are focusing on veggies."

"Charlie had mentioned that. She gave me a basket full."

"I love her. We went to school together."

"Nice."

I handed her the check as we'd agreed on. "Thank you so much for introducing yourself at the feed store yesterday. This has made it seamless."

"I'm so happy that I was in the right place at the right time. Keep in touch and don't hesitate to reach out with questions. I've been at this for years and years. Plus, I always have babies of some kind or another, so as you settle in with these, give me a call. I might have donkeys soon and I have ducklings nearly hatched."

"I'll keep that in mind."

We hugged and then I hopped in my truck to drive my new babies home. Thankfully, it was a short five miles from door to door, but I still went slowly, so I didn't shake them up too much. Plus, I was still getting used to the truck.

I pulled as close to the barn as I could. Misty came running out of the house, through the newly installed dog door. She ran to me and then to the trailer.

"Can you smell our new babies?"

She wagged her tail. She whimpered a little in what I could only guess was excitement.

First, I got out the chickens and got them settled in. They seemed happy enough as they peeped and explored their new space. I double checked the temperature.

Honestly, I was more concerned that it would be too warm out for them rather than too cold at this point, which is why I wanted to keep them in the more controllable barn. It would give them and me a chance to get comfortable, and let their little bodies get better at regulating their temperature before putting them in the coop. They would grow fast and likely move out in a week or two.

It would likely be an activity for my first guests, but I was going to play that by ear.

Next, I went and got the two pigs. They were a bit scared, and I had a bit of trouble with them, but once I got them in their pen, they seemed happy. They began exploring right away. I checked they had water and that their mud pit hadn't dried out too much in the Texas heat.

"Good to go, little pigs." I turned back to the trailer and for the hardest part. Five baby goats.

I reached over and grabbed two of them, carried those two to the enclosure and then went back for two more. Then finally, the last little one. She was bleating and carrying on.

"Oh, I'm sorry, little one. You probably thought I'd forgotten you." I pet and talked to her as I carried her to join the rest of the herd.

When I set her down, she looked at me once and then ran off to join the others. I watched them greet each other and bounce around. They began climbing on all the platforms and toys I had built in the yard for them. Goats needed to be kept busy with climbing and jumping.

I looked over to where the pigs were. They looked happy as they rolled in the mud pit and began rooting around.

I checked all the water and food once more, then scanned my property. It was really coming together. My little garden was about a month old now and looked wonderful with all the new plants.

"You know, Misty-girl, this little farm is coming along all right. What do you think?"

She wagged her tail and gave a little yip.

"So, we agree."

Now, if the ghost stays at bay, we'll be good. After watching the babies for a while, I headed inside to get my dinner going and then settle in for the night.

I was startled awake by a voice, his voice. Even in my slumbered-confusion, I knew it was him. A fog engulfed me, and I felt his ghostly grip tighten around my throat and I couldn't move, just like when he had grabbed in the hallway that one day. The icy chill of his touch went right through to my soul.

A blood-curdling scream came as if from the depth of me. It was a fear I could feel in my bones. This was no normal fear, this was pure terror.

Misty barked and snapped at the air, but it did little good.

"Shut that dog up, Anna-Rose." His hand seemed to tighten to the point that I couldn't breathe any longer.

"I can't... I'm not..." I stuttered out.

He squeezed harder, then screamed in my face before disappearing. The fog cleared and my ability to breathe returned, though slowly. I coughed and rubbed my throat, trying to process what had happened.

Misty came to me, licking my face, and then snuggling against me. I wrapped my body around her as the tears began.

He was evil. In reading Anna-Rose's journals, I had read page after page, and account after account about the abuse she'd endured. If that was even an ounce of what she had to go through, my heart ached for her soul.

I really had to figure out how to get rid of him if I was going to be successful at my business.

Chapter Eighteen: Anna-Rose (1883)

After losing the first baby, I have now lost two more. He beat me each time I got pregnant. Next time, I won't tell him.

But with each loss, he cares for me for that day and then ignores me for a week or two, until the abuse starts again. I do not know what I hate most. The mixed signals or the abuse.

The unpredictable nature of his behavior had me on edge and depressed. He would be fine at breakfast, but by evening supper, he was a beast.

People in town were noticing. When I would make my twice a month trip to the general stores, I heard the whispers or when I'd go to church. They tried to be friendly, smile, and say how do you do? But they were all judging me.

The pastor continued to give sermons about how the wife needed to obey the husband or submit to the husband. I wanted to march to the front and tell him the rest of the verses he was not sharing. But that wouldn't be proper, and mother taught me to be a proper lady.

However, being out here in Texas, it was tough on a good day to be proper. If something didn't give soon, I was going to forget my upbringing and give in to the wild west attitude most seemed to have.

James had recently hired a few ranch hands to help him. He couldn't keep up with the cattle and had already lost about a dozen. Losing them had set off a beating that had me miscarrying my last baby and skipping church for two weeks while I healed.

I think he broke my ribs on that one. It still hurt months later.

Why he took his stress and mistakes out on, I'd never know. It wasn't just with his fists, either. He became even more aggressive in the bed. I was unhappy. My body was numb.

Though hiring the ranch hands lessened his workload, it increased mine. I had to cook the mid-day meal for five instead of just us two.

Despite being a bit more work, it was nothing I couldn't handle. I had gotten tougher and more efficient at my work. It was more of a matter that I just plain didn't want to.

The workers were always appreciative, thanking me for the meal, which would earn me a raised eyebrow from James. He never said anything, though.

Today I had butchered two chickens that I had stewed with tomatoes, onions, and carrots. Along with bread, it should fill up the men and still allow me to have some for our evening meal without having to cook something new.

I set the table and then heard them cleaning up as I started to plate their food. James was always served first and was offered the largest helping, but I ensured all the men were full before heading back out to the fields and the cattle.

"Thank you again, Mrs. Collins. This was just like my Ma used to make me." Earl said. "Gosh, I miss home cooked food."

"You're welcome." I mumbled, but I kept my eyes down.

"It was good," James said. His tone held a bit of coolness to it.

I looked up and smiled at him, which won me a rare smile from him. *Please let today be a calm day.*

Once the men were gone, I cleaned up, then brought laundry in from the line. I inhaled the fresh scent as I folded each item. It was one of my joys here. The fresh smell of the laundry.

Life was slow here. If not for James, I would be happy. The beauty of the land, the fresh, open air. But without knowing if he would hurt me that day, I couldn't fully enjoy it.

After the laundry was brought in, I began preparing supper. I wanted to add a gravy to the chicken and vegetables so it would be a little different. I got out some of our cheese to add to the bread and then cut him a large piece of cake. He didn't have sweets often, but he loved cake.

I had everything set as I heard the men leaving for the day and James was getting washed up at the outside pump. He came in with a smile. This was the James that I'd fallen in love with, but I knew the dangerous one just under the surface, so I stayed cautious.

"I have supper ready." I smiled.

"Thank you." He had a seat but didn't start eating right away. He just looked at me.

"Is everything okay?" I squirmed under his stare.

"Yes, this looks wonderful. I was thinking about how blessed I am. You are a wonderful woman, and I was lucky to find you." He seemed sincere, but I didn't believe him.

"Oh, James." I pretended to be modest when what I really felt was disgust.

"No, I mean it. I haven't been kind to you these past months, but I realize it was the stress of running all this." He gestured around. "Hiring those three men was the best thing I've done, besides asking you to marry me, of course."

He came around to me, pulling me to him for a passionate kiss. I tried to be open to it, but my body remained stiff.

He sighed. "I don't blame you for being upset with me. I'll do better by you, Anna-Rose. From this moment forward, I will."

He slapped his hand down on the table, causing me to jump, but no fist came my direction. He simply went back to his meal.

I was left speechless and with no appetite. I tried to eat, but I didn't taste any of it. He showered me with compliments throughout the entire meal, which made me uncomfortable. He had always been stoic and brooding during meals.

"Can I help you with clean-up?" He asked when he was finished.

"Oh, um, thank you, but I can handle it. I know you still need to do the evenin' chores. This one is mine." I smiled, "But thank you."

"Okay. I'll be back shortly." He hung his head as he left.

I felt awful turning down his help, but I didn't know if it came with strings attached. Would he expect something in return?

I scrapped my food for the pigs and then washed the dishes. I was drying the last when he came back. He came over and put his arms around me, then spun me around.

He began humming a tune and leading me around the room in a waltz.

I couldn't help it. I laughed. "What did you get into?"

"Love with my wife is all."

I joined him in humming the tune as we continued to dance around the room. This is what I thought life would be like for us. Perhaps he had been worried and overworked before and now he would be the James I'd falling for last year.

"Let me add a log to the fire." He whispered, twirling me and letting go, just long enough to add to the fire.

It was Saturday, so I would bath before church tomorrow. We had the water getting warm by the fire.

We would also read together before bed. Since James had gotten help around the farm, he wasn't going to bed as early any longer. It gave me time to do mending and read.

We both enjoyed reading. Mark Twain, Oscar Wilde, and Thomas Hardy were a few favorites. I had also found Louisa May Alcott quite good. Tonight, I would read from the bible as I had church tomorrow. It had been my routine my entire life to read the bible on Saturday night.

The water was ready, so I filled the tub. I had a rose scented soap that I enjoyed. I got my softest towel and then stripped for my bath.

"Can I help you?" James said, his voice husky and soft.

"Um. Thank you." I handed him my rag and soap.

The rose scent filled the air as he lathered it before beginning to wash me. He was gentle and took his time. When he had lathered my body completely, he dipped my head carefully to get my hair wet, before lathering it.

I was stunned by how gentle and caring he was being. My mind was on guard, but my heart wanted this more than anything. A lump formed in my throat as I was overcome with emotions.

Once he was satisfied with the cleanliness of my hair, he put the soap aside.

"Ready for the rinse?"

"Yes." I could barely say the word.

He scrubbed his hands into my hair to release the soap from it. I moaned slightly. It felt incredible. I craved this type of affection and intimacy with my partner, my husband. He smiled as he helped me to sit up.

"Done?"

"Yes. Thank you." I stood and leaned to grab the towel, but he took it and began drying me.

Our eyes were locked through this entire process. Once he was done, he held his hand to help me from the tub.

"Will you wash me?"

"Yes."

He stripped and climbed in. I got the second bar of soap that he used for bathing. It was not rose scented, but just plain. He chuckled when he saw it.

"Don't want me smelling like a rose?" His deep chuckle caused me to smile.

"I didn't think you would enjoy that." I teased.

I followed the same steps he had done with me. Just as he had been, I was gentle and slow. Then rinsed his body with care. When he stood, I couldn't help but noticed he was aroused. I was not surprised, though I was more surprised by my own feelings.

I dried him and then he stepped out of the tub.

"Let me dump this out for you." He picked up the tub and took it out back without bothering to put on clothing.

I giggled, watching him, naked, struggling to lift the heavy tub, but it was something he did most weeks for me. He was a strong man. The weeks that I did it, I had to use the pot I had warmed the water in to take out a pot full at a time. It took me forever.

I turned to put the soap away and hang up the towels to dry. He came back without the tub. It would be rinsed tomorrow and left out to dry.

He took me in his arms, kissing me and then took my hand leading me to the bedroom. It was the first night that I didn't cry after, the first night that I realized what my dear friend Maribeth had been gushing about. It had been pure bliss.

Why couldn't it be this way every day?

Chapter Nineteen: Lindsey (June Present Day)

I paced around as I waited for my first house guests to arrive. I'd already checked and double checked the rooms to ensure that everything was ready. Now I was standing in the foyer at my check-in counter. I turned to look at my business license and my food services license proudly displayed behind me on the wall.

"This is real!" I did a little dance.

Next, I looked over the menu for the weekend. I had everything bought and ready to be cooked. Then I reviewed the activities I had planned for them.

"Plant care. Animal care. Chicks moving to the coop." I giggled as I read the list again. Now if only James would stay away. *Please, stay away.*

The sound of gravel crunching brought me skipping back to the foyer.

"The guests!" I clapped and opened the door to greet them. "Hello, welcome."

"Hello." They called back as they got out of their car with a stretch.

It was a family of five. The oldest child looked to be about twelve. She rolled her eyes and made a groaning sound as she looked around.

The parents exchanged a look. The younger two bounced out just as Misty came around the corner, tail wagging.

"A dog!" They both yelled and dropped in front of her. She licked them all over before I could even jump to stop her.

I hadn't seen her with children yet, so this was the perfect introduction. She was doing beautifully.

"She's the welcoming committee."

"She is doing a good job." Said the older boy as Misty licked his face. He giggled and hugged her.

The adults chuckled.

"Can I help you with bags or anything?"

"I think we can get it." The dad said. "I'm Zane. This is my wife, Hilary. Our oldest is Paige. Then we have Colt and Lily."

"Nice to meet you all. I'm Lindsey and this is Misty."

They grabbed bags and included the kids in carrying their own. Misty followed closely as we all made our way inside.

"Wow, your home is gorgeous." Hilary said, stepping in. "I love this wallpaper. Vintage?"

"Yes, well patterned after it anyway. Thank you."

I went through the check-in process by first confirming the number of days they would stay, then that they had rented three of the rooms. I didn't mention it to them, but I hadn't rented the fourth room. That gave them privacy for the weekend.

"I will give you a quick tour once we finish the check in. We will have three meals served, but you are also welcome to go into town to eat at the local diner anytime. Just please let me know in advance so I can plan. Here is a schedule of activities."

Hilary stuck her hand out quickly for it, so I handed it to her with a smile. She quickly scanned the list.

"This looks like fun. Look kids, we will get to learn about farm animals."

She pointed to the item on the list as she held it for the kids to read. I smiled as I realized my dream was coming true right in front of my eyes.

"Yay! What kind do you have?"

"Well, besides Misty, I have baby goats, chicks, and two pigs. I will add more soon. I am currently waiting for some ducks to hatch. Once they do, I will add a few."

"Wow!" the two younger ones said as they looked at each other and giggled.

"Alright. I think that is all the boring stuff. Now for the quick tour. You can leave your bags here while I show you the downstairs area, then we can grab them before heading upstairs."

We stepped into the living room area.

"This is the living room, obviously. You can use this room until 8 pm each night and starting at 6 am each morning."

"Do you have a television?" Paige asked.

"No, I don't."

"Not at all?" She blurted. "What do you even do?"

"I have Wi-Fi, but it can be spotty."

That was probably the stupidest answer ever. I didn't even get to tell her all the fun things I had planned or about the horseshoes set up outside, or the stacks of board games. Plus, I thought the animals were a lot of fun, and I spent most of my time outside.

Paige crossed her arms hard.

"She'll be fine. I'm sure there will be lots to do around here." Zane's voice was firm and aimed towards his oldest. She rolled her eyes again in reply, but didn't say a word.

I smiled, then continued the downstairs tour. Once done, we headed back to the foyer, grabbed their bags, and then headed upstairs to finish the tour by showing them their rooms.

"I don't have any other guests, so you can use any of the four rooms up here, plus two bathrooms. For you," I turned towards Zane and Hilary, "I recommend this one here. It has a beautiful view of the sunrise in the morning." I pointed to toward the window. They peeked out and smiled.

"This looks perfect." Hilary said.

"Great, then for the kiddos, these two have a good view of the barnyard from here." I gestured to the two middle rooms.

The two little ones flew to the window.

"Oh, you can see the pigs and the goats from here." Colt squealed. Lily bounced up and down, giggling.

Paige slowly moved toward the window and leaned over her siblings. Her mouth twitched as she watched the babies run around and play in the yard. It was almost a smile.

Hilary and Zane looked at each other, sharing a sweet, silent exchange.

"Well, I will let you all settle in. I'll be outside if you need me. Come on, Misty." I waved as I left the room with the dog at my side.

I practically floated down the stairs and out to the barnyard. My dream was no longer a dream. It was reality.

As I reached the barnyard, my babies came running toward me.

"Hi, babies." I climbed over the fence. I started raking up the yard before the guests came out. "Y'all are some messy babies."

That won me a round of bleats and oinks. I filled water bowls and added more to the pigs' mud hole. Then I added fresh hay and alfalfa pellets to the troughs. I grabbed a brush and started brushing them. They really didn't need it, but they liked it. It was good for bonding.

Suddenly, Misty barked and ran out toward the back of the house, just as Colt and Lily came running out, followed by smiling parents and a sulking sister.

"Hi, can we come in there too?" Lily asked.

"Yes, but first, you can't move quickly around them, okay? They are still babies and can scare easily."

"Okay, we'll be careful." Colt said, as he started to climb the fence.

"Here, let me open the gate for you." I picked up a rogue goat that tried to make a run for it when I opened the gate.

My guests joined me, and my tiny herd immediately swarmed the little kids. As the children giggled and pet the goats, mom and dad took pictures. I smiled, enjoying the moment. This was exactly how I pictured this all going. It was beautiful.

Now, if I could get James Collins under control, I could live like this forever.

"What are their names?" Paige asked.

"You know, I haven't named them yet. Do y'all want to help me name them?"

That won me cheers from Colt and Lily, and a smile from Paige. They began throwing out names, but I couldn't hear all of them at the same time.

They finally agreed on the pigs being Cinnamon and Sugar.

"Why Sugar?" Hilary asked them. "It's not white."

"Because they are red, so this one is Cinnamon and Sugar goes with Cinnamon." Colt said, and the girls agreed.

"Well, okay. Cinnamon and Sugar. Now the goats." I laughed.

They couldn't decide, but they had a lot of ideas.

"Teddy!" Lily yelled.

"They're girls, stupid." Paige snapped.

"We don't call each other stupid, Paige." Hilary corrected.

"Peaches! Rose!" Lily yelled, "Oh, Lily?"

"Yes, I think one *should* be named Lily." I said. "But which one?"

She looked at each one with the older kids helping her. They settled on one of the black, gray, and white sisters.

"The other one should be Paige, since they're sisters." Colt said.

"But there are no boy animals to name after you." Lily pouted.

"That's okay." But the disappointed in his voice showed.

"Well, if one chick turns out to be a rooster, I will name him Colt. How about that?"

The kids cheered and agreed that was a great idea.

They named the other three goats Peaches, Rosie, and Midnight. It gave me the idea to let guests name future animals too. Marley had already mentioned she'd have donkeys ready soon, and of course, her ducks were hatching any day now. I couldn't wait.

After naming the animals, I gave them lessons on basic care. The children were full of questions. Lily enjoyed brushing the goats.

"Do they give milk?" Colt asked.

"Not yet, but once they are older, they will."

"They have to have babies to make milk." Paige added.

"That's right."

They were extremely smart. We then moved to where the chicks were. A few were getting feathers.

"Tomorrow, with your help, we will move all these little babies to the coop."

They oohed and awed over the babies. Paige had let down her guard and was smiling and laughing. Hilary looked over at me at one point and mouthed a thank you. I simply smiled.

The rest of their stay went well, too. They enjoyed my food, my activities, and the kids didn't even seem to notice that I had no television or spotty Wi-Fi. I had found a craft online for making bird feeders out of pinecones, peanut butter, and seeds. When it was craft time, the kids had fun hunting for pinecones.

"Here's one!" Lily yelled, as she put it in the basket that I'd let them use for collecting.

"I have another one." Colt said.

Even Paige was running around excitedly, finding them.

"This one is too small, but it sure is pretty." She held it for me to see.

"Yes, very pretty."

She threw it back but found a few more the right size.

Once they'd collected enough pine cones, we smeared them with peanut butter and rolled them in the seeds. I had added mealworms to the seed as well, which earned a *'ew, gross'* from the kids. We attached string and then hung those in the trees.

"Now, we have to wait for the birds to discover them." I said. "Who's ready for snack time?"

Everyone cheered and followed me to the porch. I went into retrieve the giant cookies that I'd baked plus the lemonade. The family sat there playing cards, eating their snack, and watching the birds eat at the feeders.

I sat in the kitchen, listening to the laughter, and smiled at my new life. This was so much better than working in a cube for people who were angry and could set you up to fail. This was all on me to succeed or fail.

Sunday afternoon rolled around after a wonderful first weekend with guests. As I was checking the family out, the children thanked me over and over for a fun weekend, even Paige. The sulking preteen had transformed into a fun-loving kid and enjoyed herself.

But my biggest win of the weekend was that James Collins' ghost never made an appearance. In fact, I hadn't heard a peep from him since that night when Misty was barking and he was choking me, somehow. I still didn't understand how that happened.

"Thank you for staying with us. I hope you will come back in the future." I called as the Becketts were loading their bags.

Lily said something to her mom and then came running back to me, throwing herself into my arms for a big hug.

"Thank you so much. It was the best weekend ever."

"I'm so glad you had fun."

She giggled and ran back to the car. Zane honked as they pulled down the long driveway and headed home. I turned back toward my house.

"Time to get ready for my next guests!"

My best friends were coming in this week for a mid-week trip and then I would have a full house with two separate families next weekend. I couldn't wait.

Chapter Twenty: Lindsey (June Present Day)

I grabbed the empty bottle of wine and carried it to the kitchen, dropping it in the recycle bin and then grabbed a fresh one. My girlfriends had arrived earlier today, and we had the best day.

We had enjoyed my famous Bolognese with pasta, salad, and homemade bread for dinner. Now we were catching up over drinks on my back porch.

"Simone, you are so bad," Bailey was saying through a laugh.

"What did I miss?" I sat and started topping everyone's glasses off.

"You remember that lady at work who kept stealing my lunch?"

"Yeah?"

"I might have treated her to a bit of a laxative two weeks ago." Simone added with a giggle.

"Ohmygosh! You didn't?"

"I did. She was out for two days. My lunch hasn't disappeared since."

"Couldn't you get in trouble for that?" Rachel asked.

"Maybe, but she was stealing my lunch every single day, even after I caught her doing it." Simone sat up. "Why my lunch?"

"She should be fired."

"She's sleeping with the CEO."

"No way!" Bailey slapped her thigh. "Then she deserves the lax lunch."

"Damn straight." Simone laughed.

"Anna-Rose."

"Crap." I said, as a cold sweat came over me.

"What was that?" Rachel asked.

"Is that the ghost you told me about?" Simone asked.

"What ghost? You didn't tell me about a ghost." Bailey grabbed her wine and chugged it.

"Yeah, he has been quiet for days. I thought maybe he had moved along."

"Anna-Rose!" He called out and I could hear the creak of his footsteps moving through his house.

"Is he coming this way?" Bailey said, jumping up.

"I think so."

More stomping footsteps and his demand for Anna-Rose to show herself.

"He sounds angry." Bailey's voice trembled.

We all stood and faced the house. Misty ran in and started barking. I heard the voice curse and then the house went quiet. Misty came back wagging her tail.

"Did you get rid of the mean spirit?" I dropped in front of my dog, hugging and scratching her. "Good girl."

"Your dog has superpowers." Rachel said.

"What am I going to do about this spirit? I have to get rid of him."

"What's his deal?" Simone asked.

"Remember how I told you about how I look like this Anna-Rose?"

"That's the name he kept saying." She frowned.

"Yeah. That was his wife."

"What?" the group collectively gasped.

"Yeah. I need to dig out the pictures that I have of her and show y'all."

"I can't get over this y'all thing." Simone laughed as she plodded down into her chair.

"I know. I've fallen right into life here."

Rachel's phone chimed, signaling that her family needed her. That was the end of her being part of the conversation for the rest of the evening.

The rest of us settled back to our seats with our wine and changed the subject. We didn't get back to the ghost again. Thankfully, he always seemed deterred by Misty. I wonder if I should get a second dog.

The next morning, I woke before my friends and started making thick maple bacon and crisp, fluffy waffles. I had fresh strawberries and blueberries to top them with. I also started the coffee to brew.

Once the smells started to fill the room and make their way upstairs, I heard my friends stir. Simone was the first to join me.

"Oh, this smells incredible in here." She grabbed a mug and filled it with the house blend coffee from Jack's Beans. She then took a seat at my kitchen island. "I love all of this for you. You look so happy."

"I feel happy. Happier than I have in... years."

"I'm so glad. I was worried about you coming all this way without anyone."

"Yeah, it probably seemed crazy, but I honestly feel like I'm at home here. Like I belong here."

She was quiet for a moment, then took a sip of coffee.

"Okay, I have something crazy to ask." She said after a moment.

"I would expect nothing less."

"Ha, ha. But seriously. This Anna-Rose person, you said you look like her?"

"Yeah, oh my gosh, I need to show you the pictures later. Remind me." I flipped the slices of bacon and took a waffle out of the maker.

"Okay, well, hear me out on this. What if you *are* her?"

"What?" I laughed.

"No, seriously. You're an old soul. What if your soul was her?" She took a sip of coffee. "That would explain her husband haunting you, right? You said he has gotten... angry with you."

"Yeah." I was skeptical but listening.

"Didn't you tell me the rumor was that she killed him? What if he abused her, and that's why she killed him, *AND* he has just been waiting to get back at her or you?" She swiped a piece of bacon and bit into it while I felt as if I'd been gut-punched.

He had abused her. I had read it all, but I hadn't gotten to the part of her journal where he dies.

"Well, crap. What do I do with that?"

"I don't know, but maybe you need to find one of those mediums or someone who can get rid of him?"

"Yeah. I need to look into that for sure. I can't live with this guy or ghost or whatever. And yes, he abused her. Brenda, from the library, gave me those journals. I read it in there."

"You did? You didn't tell me that."

"A lot has happened."

"We need to go through those. Maybe there is an answer in them."

Rachel and Bailey joined us then, so we changed the subject. I know Bailey is scared easily. Rachel was already texting. She mumbled about the dishwasher.

"Do y'all want to go with me to pick out my next animals? I'm supposed to get ducks and a couple of donkeys."

Bailey squealed a yes while the other two were not as enthusiastic.

"I'm so glad that you love all this farm life, Linds, but that's not my thing." Rachel said, getting a cup of coffee and a plate of food.

"I'll go, but only because I love you." Simone added.

While all the ladies were my friend, Simone had been my very best friend since I first moved to California. She had originally been the girlfriend of one of Derek's friends. We met at a party and bonded over our hatred for one of the other girlfriends who, as it turned out, we were right about. She was a gold digger and ended up taking everything from the man.

"If he didn't see it for himself, there was nothing we could have done to stop it." Simone had said.

"It was so obvious." I'd agreed.

Simone broke up with her boyfriend a few months later, but we had remained friends since. She had held my hand through my miscarriages and all the low moments that followed.

She ended up dating another one of Derek's friends, and he worked with Derek's father at some tech company.

"I love you and appreciate your sacrifice." I stuck my tongue out at her, causing her to throw her napkin at me.

We wrapped up breakfast, then I went to feed all my animals and let them out of the barn. Bailey joined me happily while the other two dragged their feet. Rachel, mostly, because her cell phone kept buzzing.

"I just love all these babies. They are so cute." She giggled, giving a handful of pellets to Lily Goat, as I had started to call her.

I couldn't get the human Lily's sweet face out of my head. Had my first baby lived, it would have been about Lily's age. At 39, I was hearing the clock tick on my viable fertile years. Maybe I should consider freezing my eggs.

Even with the pain in my heart, I was glad to at least have a goat named for the little spunky girl who had been one of my first guests. The goat would be a reminder.

"They are fun, but a lot of work." I said.

"I don't know how you get anything done. I would end up playing with them more than work."

"Ha, then you'd be no good at this bed-and-breakfast thing."

"You make it look easy." She leaned over and gave me a side-hug.

We finished up with the animals and then went to get ready for our trip to Marley's farm. I hooked up the trailer, my friends piled into the truck, and then I told Misty I'd be right back.

"You watch the house, good girl." I gestured my hand back, and she went up on the porch to watch me depart. She had been so easy. I can't get over that she had been abandoned.

We made the short drive to my new friend's farm.

"Wow, this is amazing." Simone said, when we pulled down the driveway. "Is this what your place will look like one day?"

"Gosh, I hope so. Isn't it amazing?"

Animals ran and frolicked in their various pens and yards as far as the eye could see. Her crops were far more mature than what I had. She ran a small stand to sell them at. She wasn't set up as a bed-and-breakfast like I was, but she was a hot spot for all the locals for fresh produce, meats, and pets.

She stepped out of one of the barns and waved.

"Howdy, Lindsey." She said, stepping forward once I was parked.

"Good morning. I want to introduce you to my friends." I turned as they stepped out of the truck. "This is Simone, Rachel, and Bailey. They are visiting me from California."

"Nice to meet you, ladies." She smiled at each of them. They returned her greeting. "Well, let me show you the donkeys cuz I know you've been dying to get your hands on them."

I laughed, "I can't wait."

We walked to a corral that I couldn't see from the driveway. It was full of tiny donkeys.

"Like I told you, these are our minis. They will be about the size of a dog, well, like your Misty, maybe bigger."

"They are so cute!" Bailey gushed. "How will you pick?"

"I'll just know."

"Are you going to stick with girls again?"

"No, I think I'm getting at least one boy. I promised a sweet little boy that I would name one after him." Though I know I had promised him it would be a rooster, but I had a feeling he would like this better.

Everyone asked at once who, what, when.

"My first guests were this great family. Paige, Colt, and Lily were the children. The girls named two of the goats, the two sisters, Paige and Lily, so I promised Colt my first boy would be named after him. Hillary, the mom, asked if I could send a picture once I had him."

"And that's how you build a relationship with customers." Simone chuckled.

"Maybe I listened to you a few times." I bumped my shoulder into hers. "Alright, which ones are boys?"

Marley started pointing to them, and I got the hang of checking them myself.

"How about that little guy? The light gray there."

"Oh, he's a good one. Big personality, smart. He will keep you on your toes, but I think will be a great pet." Marley went to get him for me.

He happily followed her over to us. She moved him into a smaller pen. I went in with him to greet him. He was friendly, nibbling at my shirt and nudging my hand for pets.

"Alright, Colt, you are definitely coming home with me." I snapped a couple of pictures that I sent off to Hilary with a note for the human Colt. The reply was almost instant. Human Colt was extremely happy. Hilary confirmed they were planning another trip to visit before the end of Summer.

I can't wait. I replied.

"Okay, so I have a few non-related females in case you want to breed them." She started pointing them out.

I picked out a reddish-brown with a white face and then a spotted one who just screamed happiness.

"She will be named Happy and this one will be, well, I don't know yet. Maybe I'll let my next guests pick her name."

"What about us?" Bailey asked.

"Of course, yes, y'all can pick her name."

My friends whispered back and forth, but then tabled it for now. We moved from the donkeys to the incubator with the ducks.

"Most of them will be ready to go in the yard pretty much now, but if you want to acclimate them, keep them in your barn for a few days to a week, like you did with the chickens."

"Alright. Sounds good."

I picked out a dozen of the Runner ducks. I had never heard of the breed, but she showed me the adults and I fell in love. They didn't fly but run everywhere. I couldn't wait to see them fully grown.

"Next time, you'll need to get mini cows!" Marley said, pointing to a corral in the distance.

"I need to have a new barn built. This here will max me out."

"I can give you some recommendation for good contractors, and Frank is always happy to help."

"I used Sullivan Construction for some of the work in my house."

"Oh, well, Greg is the best! You should be good then." She smiled.

We loaded up my new babies and headed home. I was so excited about my farm coming together.

"That wasn't as bad as I thought it would be," Simone said, on the drive home.

"See? This is fun."

"I wouldn't go that far." She laughed.

When they went home, I was going to miss them. I still hadn't gotten out as much as I would have liked here. I had been so focused on getting my house and business up and running that I had only met a few people so far.

I couldn't imagine Molly or June or Marley being like these ladies, though. These were my ride or die friends.

But I hoped to fix my friendship status here in Wisteria, as I would attend my first town festival in just a few days. It would be the Summer Festival that they combined with the Fourth of July. I would have guests staying, and had it marked as a planned activity for the day. I couldn't wait.

The next morning, I drove the ladies the two hours back to the airport. We cried as we said goodbye.

"I'll be back to visit again soon." Simone whispered. "Oh, and I'll research your pest problem."

"Thank you."

I waved as they went into the airport and back to their lives far away. I sighed as I pulled away from the curb. It had been a good few days with them here, but I needed to get refocused on my new life.

Chapter Twenty-One: Lindsey (July Present Day)

My friends left yesterday and today I would have a day care come out to visit the farm and the town's reporter was coming as well. They were going to do a piece on my farm and take pictures for the town museum. Brenda was going to join them for the visit.

"We rarely close the library, but today is a special occasion." She had said when they called to confirm the appointment.

I didn't have guests until tomorrow, so it was the perfect day for it. Once I'd dropped my friends off at the airport, I spent the rest of the day cleaning and getting ready for the interview and my upcoming weekend guests.

I was making up the last bed when I heard the familiar sound of a car driving up. I peeked out the window and saw Brenda, along with a few people I didn't know.

"Wait a minute, is that the mayor?" I didn't know she was coming. I checked my reflection in the mirror and smoothed my blouse before sprinting down the stairs to greet my guests.

"Hi, good morning." I called when I stepped out of the door.

The visitors turned to smile at me. It was Brenda, the mayor, and then two others that I assumed were with the newspaper.

"Hello." Brenda stepped forward. "I would like to introduce you to Emily Freya. She's the mayor of our fine town."

"Nice to meet you." Emily said, stepping forward to shake my hand.

"Nice to meet you as well."

"Then, we have Sunday Livingston and Amber Lee. They both work for the paper. Amber will take pictures and Sunday will do the interview."

"Nice to meet you both and welcome to Evans Bed-and-Breakfast." I smiled. "Do you want to start with the house or the yard?"

They looked around. Sunday and Amber exchanged a few looks.

"The house, please." Sunday finally said.

"Great. Come on in."

We stepped into the foyer area. It was the first thing guests saw coming in. It was cute and cozy, but still professional.

"Oh, wow, this is so adorable." Emily said. "I had come in here a few times growing up, but it never looked this good."

"Can we get a few pictures of you behind the counter there?" Amber directed. "We'll start out posed, but then maybe some casual ones."

"Okay." I stepped behind the counter and posed as she directed while the other three looked on.

"Good, good. Now pretend you are working on the computer. Yes. Perfect. Alright. Thanks."

"So, what made you choose this wallpaper? It's gorgeous." Sunday asked with her pen at the ready.

"I wanted to give a nod to the original owners and the days when they lived here." I looked at it. "I believe, from what I've learned about here over the past few months, that Anna-Rose would have loved this."

There were a few bumps and creaks above us. All heads turned toward the sound.

"And how are you dealing with the ghost?" Sunday asked. Her voice wavered a bit.

"Um, it's mostly just bumps and thumps. He doesn't seem to like the dog."

Everyone looked down at Misty.

She wagged her tail in response to the attention. I didn't mention my more violent encounters with him, no reason to get bad press. Sometimes bad press was just that, bad.

"Yeah, I've heard a few things myself," Brenda said. "You know, most everyone in town has spent some time out here, usual as a teen looking for trouble."

The group laughed. Several folks had told me the same thing. It was definitely a popular hangout.

"I've heard that several times."

"Well, let's see the rest of this masterpiece." Brenda said.

They followed me into the living room, dining room area, and then the kitchen. Amber had me pose a few times, but she also took some of just the rooms.

"I love how you found that shiplap. It is gorgeous on that accent wall."

It was on the shared wall between the living room and foyer. I had stained it dark and then did a whitewash over it. It gave it an aged look.

"Thanks. That was a good find. Most of the walls looked to have old plaster or drywall in the newer section. I replaced it all."

They followed me upstairs. More pictures. Sunday rapid firing questions while Amber snapped from every angle. The mayor and Brenda chatted about this detail or that.

"Oh, wait, I recognize this. Was this in the attic?" Brenda asked.

It was one of the ceramic figurines that I had found in the trunks.

"Yes, it was. In fact, it was in one of these trunks." I pointed to the one in this room. I was using it to store extra blankets and linens.

"These are lovely. Anna-Rose would be so pleased. I mean, I didn't know her, of course, but learning about her from my grandmother, as I told you. She wanted some of her things to live on, and they are." Brenda smiled.

Amber took pictures of the items while Sunday made a note of them.

Once we had toured the entire house, we moved outside, starting with my favorite place in the world, the back porch.

"Each day, I serve the guests an afternoon snack here on the porch. There are games in those cabinets there."

"This is beautiful." Emily said as she sat to take in the view.

Amber had me pose and then had Brenda and Mayor Emily join me. She had us pull out some cards so we could pretend to play. Sunday was making notes and asking questions.

"What kind of snacks do you serve? Is this every day or just certain days?"

"It depends on the guest. When they register, I have a short questionnaire that I have them fill out. It just gives me an idea of any food allergies and then likes and dislikes. Then I serve based on the guest. My first guests, a family of five, got giant cookies and lemonade the first day, then the next I cut up fruit and veggies with iced tea and flavored water. I had a girl's trip here the past few days, and they got a charcuterie board and wine one day, then scones and tea the next."

I didn't mention that those were my friends, and they had asked for those things specifically.

"Oh, nice. I love it." Emily said. "Maybe I should book a couple of days out here with my family."

"I'd love to have you."

Misty ran into the house, barking. At her barks, my blood ran cold. That's how she would bark when James would be creeping around. Then I heard the creaks and pops, then a curse.

All eyes turned from the house to me. I shrugged.

"He doesn't like dogs."

"The ghost?" Sunday asked.

"Um, yeah." Crap, I didn't want them to focus on this. I tried to laugh it off. "Maybe he is more of a cat person."

Nervous laughter from the group.

"So, um, I have some of my famous giant cookies and iced tea, if you would like. I can bring it out here as we finish up."

"That sounds lovely." Brenda and the mayor said at the same time.

"Great, just give me a moment."

I came back inside, trying to compose myself. I really wanted to give a tongue-lashing to a certain spirit. He scared me though, so I probably couldn't tell him off.

I worked quickly to pour the iced teas, plate the cookies, then ensuring I had all the special touches like sliced lemons and local honey for the tea. I put store-bought napkins in a stack next to a few of the floral printed plates I'd found in the attic. It looked picture perfect.

I carried the tray out, pushing through the swinging back screen door.

"Here we go." I said, setting the tray in front of Brenda and Emily.

"Oh, this is lovely." Emily clapped her hands.

"What a beautiful tray." Brenda leaned forward to look.

"Is this a good representation of an afternoon snack?" Sunday asked.

The snap of the camera was Amber's reply. I smiled.

"Yes, this is how I normally serve it."

"Oh, this is from the Jenkins farm." Emily said, noting the honey.

"It is."

"And these were Anna-Rose's plates. I recognize her pattern." Brenda picked one up, studying the floral print.

We ate the cookies, and they shared stories about the house or their life in Wisteria. I listened. I loved learning about everyone here. As we wrapped up the snack, we heard the day care van pulling down the driveway.

"Oh, the day care must be here." I said.

This was a day care from a neighboring town. They weren't a farm focused town like Wisteria. From my conversation with the director, most of the kids hadn't had a lot of hands-on experience with farm animals or gardening. Well, today I was hoping to change that for all of them.

We all walked around to the front of the house to greet them. The plan was to take more pictures with the children here. We had all the parents sign a release. Those that didn't have a release would not have pictures taken. I had an activity table set up, so we would move the children between the various things, but they would be grouped by permission and no permission.

"Hi, are you Judy?" I greeted one lady.

"Yes, that's me, and this is Gia, and then all the kiddos."

"Nice to meet you all."

I watched as the kids disembark the van and stood in a somewhat straight, though bouncy line. They giggled as they waited patiently. A few wiggled their fingers at me in a cute sort of greeting.

Once everyone was lined up. Gia and Judy turned to me.

"We have gone over some rules, but do you have any special ones?"

"Yes, we don't run around the animals. They might run around, but they get scared sometimes with people they don't know well. Only feed them food I give you. And do not go in any parts of the barn with doors closed." I thought. "Oh, and don't open the gate without an adult. I have a few goats that try to break out every time I open it."

The kids giggled.

Amber asked about which could be photographed and which ones couldn't.

"All the parents signed off as yes, so we are all good."

"Oh, that's great. Makes my job that much easier."

"Well, then let me show you to the good stuff." I said, gesturing for them to follow me.

We walked straight to the barnyard, where all the animals came to greet us. I had them go into the barn area because I could close the outside gate and then open the inside one, so we didn't have any escaping animals.

Once inside, I started handing out cups of pellets and brushes.

"Does anyone know any facts about any of these animals?" I asked.

Kids all around me started yelling things. Some were true, but some were not. All were cute. I didn't correct those that were wrong, I simply gave facts.

"Goats can give milk. We get bacon from pigs. Chickens lay eggs."

They asked what the names were.

"Well, the chickens and ducks don't have names yet, but the goats, pigs, and donkeys do." I started giving the names.

"Oh, I love the name Lily."

"Why is the red pig named sugar? Sugar is white, not red."

"Rosie is cute."

"My baby brother's name is Colt."

The goats got bored with the children and started climbing and jumping from their platforms and bridges. The children laughed, pointed, and a few tried to follow them.

"Aiden, that's not for people," Judy corrected.

The mayor, Brenda, and Sunday watched from the shade, chatting back and forth. Amber kept the camera snapping. Judy and Gia were kept quite busy by the children. They were going in twelve different directions.

"I have a craft, if you think they would be interested?" I said to Gia.

"They might." She rounded them up, and they all agreed to do the craft.

It was a nature tree painting. I gave each child a small basket so they could collect items from the yard. I had printed out tree trunks and we would glue the collected items to make the canopy of the trees.

"In this area here, you can find all kinds of fun things. Leaves, flowers, small rocks. Collect them and then we will make trees out of them."

The children loved the idea and were off running and collecting. It took every adult to keep them close and help them, but soon they all had enough to glue.

Amber took pictures while the rest of us helped with the glue.

"This is fun!"

"It looks so pretty."

"You're cool."

"Can I take it home?"

They were all full of questions and chatty. I tried to answer as many as I could, but they often talked over each other.

"Alright, now let's leave those to dry, and I have one more thing planned for us. Who enjoys gardening?"

Most of the hands went up, but one little boy yelled he hated it.

"My grandma makes me pick the weeds and I hate it."

"Yeah, I hate that part too, but to let the plants grow big and strong, we have to take out the weeds. Does anyone know why?"

The same boy piped up, "My grandma says they take from the other plants."

"Yes, they steal the water and food, so the other plants don't get as much."

We walked over to the garden, and they all started yelling things they recognized.

"Tomatoes. I love tomatoes."

"What is that? Broccoli. Yuck."

"I like broccoli, but didn't know it looked like that."

"What is that one? I don't see anything."

I looked over to see which one the child was pointing to. "That will be carrots. They grow under the ground."

"Uh-oh, I see weeds." The little boy pointed. "Grandma would not like that."

I tried not to laugh. As I fought that reaction, I walked over and pulled it up. He smiled. I gave them a quick tour and allowed them to each pick a few things to take with them. I had small paper sacks that I printed each name on, so they could know which was theirs.

With the activities done, they went to collect their artwork and then, in a nearly straight line, they walked back to their van. After a few hours on the farm, they were a lot less bouncy.

"What do we say to Ms. Lindsey?" Judy prompted.

"Thank you, Ms. Lindsey!"

"Well, thank y'all too. I hope you had fun."

"We did."

"Yeah!"

"I did."

"Watch out for weeds."

They loaded into the van and waved as they pulled away. I then turned towards my other guests.

"I hope y'all had fun too." I smiled. "Did you get enough for your story? Pictures?"

"I think we did."

"This is really something good you have going on here. We are so thrilled to have you here in Wisteria." Emily said, offering her hand. I shook it as I thanked her.

They then loaded into their car and left.

I stood there as I watched the dust settle on the road. It had been a good day, but James nearly ruined it.

I really hoped Sunday would leave out the part about him, but I had to admit, it could add to the interest of those in the area. Those who grew up coming out here as a teen could be my best marketers.

"Maybe bad publicity wasn't so bad after all."

Chapter Twenty-Two: Lindsey (July Present Day)

I smiled as I put a jug of tea in each picnic basket. I straightened the items inside and then ensured that the guests' names were clearly displayed on top.

Today was the Summer Festival in town. I was so excited to get to know more of my neighbors. Misty would go with me, and I'd gotten her a fun Fourth of July bandanna to wear.

The first of my guests came downstairs. They had twin boys who were eight years old. The boys loved helping me feed all the animals yesterday.

"Good morning. Are you ready for today's festival?" I asked the pair.

"Yes!" they both said.

"Can we feed the animals before we go?" Trip asked. He was the braver of the two. His twin Gage was more laid back and let Trip take the lead.

"I have already fed them today, but if you aren't too tired this evening, you can help me put them to bed."

"Yay!" they cheered.

"Here is your picnic lunch, plus a snack." I handed it to their mother, Blair. She smiled and thanked me.

The other family came down a few minutes later. It was a mom with her two teen daughters. They smiled and took their basket, commenting on how wonderful they'd slept.

I was glad to hear it because I'd slept awfully. James Collins stalked me all night. Poor Misty had paced and whined. It didn't appear that the guests were disturbed at all, which I was thankful for.

It seemed to be me he was after and if what Simone suggested was true, my soul may have once belonged to his wife, Anna-Rose. A chill ran through me.

Did I even believe in that? Nay. I shook the thought. It was ridiculous.

"Time to get out of here, Misty."

She wagged her tail and bounced around.

I grabbed our own picnic basket, my purse, and keys, then we headed out. Misty went in the backseat and went from window to window, looking out as we drove the few miles into town.

When I got close, I could see and hear the festivities. Everything was decorated in red, white, and blue, including the people. A few waved as I drove by. I could hear a marching band playing. It got my energy pumping.

"This is going to be fun."

Misty agreed.

Everyone was to park at the school. Signal pointed the way. I giggled to myself as I exited the car. I grabbed Misty's leash, but left the insulated lunch in the car for now.

We followed the crowd. The energy was intoxicating. Children laughing, giggling, skipping along. Parents talking to each other, reminding their children to watch for cars, stay close.

I smiled as everyone greeted Misty, especially children, which meant everyone we pass got a tail wag and a doggy smile.

"Oh, hey, there, Lindsey!" I heard someone call my name. I turned to find Bart and his wife; Heidi walked towards me. Misty started wagging her whole body when she saw him.

"Hey, Misty!" He dropped in front of her.

She was happy to see him, but she looked up at me to make sure I was still there, I guess. I hoped she was happy living with me.

"She looks really good. She doing okay?" Bart asked as he stood.

"Yeah, she's doing great. Acclimated really quickly to my house and routine. She's learned so much in such a short time with me."

"That's good. Oh, you remember my wife, Heidi?"

"Yes, good to see you."

"Yeah, good to see you again, too. And happy to see Misty." Heidi smiled.

We walked together to Main Street, where the booths lined the street and while the high school band played in front of city hall. We parted ways as they went to watch the band.

I went to walk around the booths. I introduced myself to the different shops and farmers as I looked for new products to use at my bed-and-breakfast.

"Oh, hey, Lindsey!" Marley's familiar voice called out. I turned to see their booth behind me.

"Hey, Marley. Hi, Frank."

"Mornin', how's the farm going?" Frank asked.

"It's great. All the babies are doing well. Growing fast. The chickens and ducks are all getting feathers. It's really cute."

"That's good to hear. I knew they were going to the right place." Marley said. "By the way, I brought bunnies today."

"Ugh, you know I'm weak when it comes to new animals" I peeked in the cages behind her. She had about a dozen little bunnies in all shades of colors. "They're so adorable."

"You need a couple for your guests to play with." Marley cooed.

"I don't have a hutch set up yet."

"I can help with that." Frank offered. "I actually have an extra one or two that we can bring over and get all set up for you. We can build a little fence around it. The works."

"That's so thoughtful, Frank. Let me think about it and I'll get back to you both."

"Okay, but they may sell out. We always do."

She always knows how to reel me in. "Okay, fine, I'll buy... two? Can you hold them until I get a hutch set up?"

"Absolutely! Which two?"

I picked out two peachy, cream-colored ones. She put a Velcro collar around each.

"That means they are sold, but it doesn't hurt them."

"You know I'm going to go broke if I keep running into you."

She laughed. "Not the way I hear it. Aren't you booked solid for months?"

It was true. I had nearly every day booked from now until late September, and then scattered days after that, but even those were getting snatched up quickly. It was a good problem to have.

"Yeah, I can't believe it. I've had to turn down bookings."

"What about that nice family, the ones that named your first animals? You'd mentioned they wanted to come back before the end of summer."

"Oh, yes, they are booked for a second trip. I'm so excited for them to see the animals since their last visit."

"And you will have that nice write up in the Wisteria Words. It will come out the day after tomorrow." Frank added.

"Yeah, that's true."

But it only went to those in town, so it wouldn't necessarily bring me a lot of business. But then I could almost hear Simone's words in my ear.

Word of mouth is the best advertising. It's free, and it is someone they trust giving them a recommendation.

She was so smart.

After I finished talking with the Jenkins, I moved to the Martin's booth. They made the best jams. I put in an order for more strawberry and fig. Then on to Suds and Soaps, and finally I came to Jack's Beans.

"Oh, hey, Lindsey," Jack said. "You haven't been in the store recently. I thought maybe you forgot us."

"Oh, hi, Jack. No, I have been there, but I didn't see you. Bree was there."

"Ah, well, you'll need to come in when I'm there. I give better discounts than Bree." He chuckled.

"I'll have to remember that."

"So, what can I get for you today?"

"I wanted to put in an order for ten pounds of the house blend."

"Of course. When do you need it?"

"Early next week works."

"Great. I'll bring by myself." He flashed his perfect teeth, dimpled smile my way.

My pulse quickened. *Yikes.*

"Perfect. I'll be home all day. With a house full of guests, I am home most days." I tried to say casually. Did it come across that way? I didn't ask.

"I've heard that you've become quite successful. Good marketing?"

"Yeah, my best friend is a marketing genius."

"Seems like it. Well, I'll bring it by Monday."

"See you then."

I felt my face warm from more than the Texas sun. Thankfully, a line was forming behind me, so it was time to move on. I smiled once more, giving an awkward wave as I moved to the next booth.

A few booths later, I bumped into Molly, literally.

"Whoops. I'm sorry... Oh, hey, Molly."

"Hey, there's my favorite former guest." She hugged me. "How've you been?"

"I'm good. We need to catch up soon. We missed our coffee this week."

"Yeah, sorry about that. Busy now with guests." I smiled. "You should visit me on my farm."

"I'd love to. I keep hearing good things." She smiled. "I'll text you?"

"That works."

"Wanna chit-chat now? I can grab us some lemonades and we can dish." She asked.

"Sounds good."

"Okay, you go claim that table before someone else does, and I'll grab us some drinks."

We split and then she came over with the lemonades and a cup of water for Misty. Misty lapped it up.

"She's a sweet dog. You got her from Bart?"

"I did. She's been the best thing." I left off the part of her being ghost repellent.

"He's a good guy. Speaking of good guys, I saw you talking to Jack."

"Oh, yeah, ordering coffee. I serve it to my guests."

"Looked like a bit more than just business."

My face warmed again. "Busted. He's kinda cute, huh?"

She looked through the crowd toward his booth. "Yeah, if you like that kind. I'm more into women, honestly."

"Oh." Not sure I was surprised exactly, but I also didn't know what to say.

"Not many singles women here that are both single and lesbians." She chuckled.

"Not many single anything here. Me, you, and maybe Jack is all I know of."

"Yeah, a couple others, but that's it." She sipped her lemonade. "So, you think you'd go out with Jack? I mean, if he asked."

Now it was my turn to look over at his booth. He looked up at that moment. Our eyes locked. He smiled and did a slight head nod my way before going back to talking to the customers at his booth.

I couldn't hide the fact there was an attraction there, and not because he was one of the few single males I knew here. Of course, I didn't get out much, so that didn't help my chances of meeting others.

"Um, yeah, I probably would."

She laughed and nudged my foot with hers. "Good."

We continued to visit. She introduced me to a few people who walked by. They commented on my business or the fact I lived in *that* haunted house. Lots of people stopped to greet Misty.

"She's so well-behaved." One lady said. "Hi, I'm Bev. I'm the school secretary."

"Oh, nice to meet you."

I made a mental note because I would likely call her to start a conversation about field trips for the kiddos. I'm sure she didn't make the decision, but maybe she could connect me to those that do.

After a while, I ran back to the car for my picnic lunch and joined Bart, Heidi, and Marley and Frank, plus Molly. The high school band played, then the choir sang. There was a speech by the mayor. She mentioned me by name and asked me to wave.

I blushed and waved to the crowd. I heard murmurs of things.

"She lives in that haunted house."

"Do you think she's seen the ghost?"

I kept my eyes down as I sat back with my friends.

After the mayor's speech, it was late afternoon. I said goodbye to my friends so I could get home to care for all the animals.

My guests had all said they were staying in town for the fireworks. I was on my own for the evening. So, after the animals were fed and secured for the night, I poured myself a glass of wine and enjoyed welcoming the evening on my back porch with a book.

"This is the life, Misty."

Her ears twitched, but she continued to sleep at my feet.

"Anna-Rose... Anna-Rose!"

"Are you kidding me? Now?" I stomped my foot. "Go away, James."

"Do not talk to me that way?" I heard him say his heavy footsteps sounded nearby, but he hadn't attacked me outside of the house, so I just stayed put.

Misty sat up, growling.

"Good girl."

The footsteps moved away until I couldn't hear them any longer, and I breathed a sigh of relief. Maybe I could manage him between being firm and keeping the dog nearby and perhaps moving my bedroom outside.

Chapter Twenty-Three: Anna-Rose (1883)

It has been several months of marital bliss. With having the extra hands here, James was happy, walking around humming tunes, being loving to me. It was exactly as I'd pictured it when I daydreamed about my life here.

Except I knew what he was capable of, so my happiness was only surface deep. Underneath, I was lonely, depressed, and angry. He had lied about who he was and was lying now.

At any moment, I knew he would be angry, especially when he found out that I was once again expecting. This time, I wouldn't tell him. He had made it clear many times that he did not want children.

"They are selfish creatures who will distract you from your household duties. Meals will be late. You won't have time for me any longer. No children." This had been practicality spat in my face a few months ago during one of his many tantrums.

After the miscarriage and his tantrum, I'd gotten a potion that would help prevent me from getting pregnant. It had been going well for several months. Though I knew it wasn't foolproof, it was my only option to protect myself and the innocent lives.

However, now I had to protect us both. It had to be drastic, and I had an idea.

"James, I was thinking, now that you have help on the farm, it might be a good time for me to travel home to visit my parents. I wouldn't be gone long, a few weeks to travel each way, and then I'll stay a week or two."

I actually planned to stay until the baby was born and then possibly stay to raise it there. It could be my escape from him and this place. Because despite our current state over the past few months, I knew this would set him off again and we would be right back to the unhappiness, beatings, and fear. Though those never were truly out of my mind.

"I don't know. I will think on it."

"Thank you."

While he thought it over, I had to come up with a back-up plan, just in case I can't escape with his blessing. Perhaps if he made another trip to Fort Worth or if he went down to Galveston like he had mentioned a few times, I could pack and leave.

When he made those trips, he was gone for nearly two weeks, so it was plenty of time for me to disappear, even if I had to walk.

It was a month before he finally gave his answer. I was getting nervous he would never give one. My stomach would get round soon. I needed to get away before that happened.

"Here." He set the train ticket in front of me.

I checked the date. It was in one month. That would put me at around four, almost five months along. I should still be able to hide this until then. I would just be careful.

"Oh, James, do you mean it? Thank you so much."

He mumbled something and then went outside to clean up before supper. He was a mystery for sure. I could live my entire lifetime and probably never understand that man.

I studied the ticket again. Just one month from now, it wouldn't matter any longer. I couldn't wait.

After supper, I wrote a letter to my parents and then got it addressed. I would make a trip to town soon to send it.

Over the next few weeks, I prepared for my trip. I ensured that there was enough food for James and the men. He said they could take turns cooking.

I had to start taking out my dresses, but I tried to do it carefully so he wouldn't notice. My stomach was still not showing through my clothing, but I couldn't let him see me without clothing. I could manage that, or so I thought. This would work.

The night before my trip, I had everything packed, and we loaded it on the wagon, well James did. I watched. The wagon was waiting in the yard to be hitched to the horses the next day.

I made a small feast for my final meal here. I told James he could eat the leftovers the next day or two, just to get him by. He grumbled something about it being a good idea.

As we got ready for bed that night, I slipped up and hadn't turned down the light enough and he saw my stomach.

"What is going on with your stomach?" He snarled. "Are you expecting?"

"What? Oh, no. I've just put on a little weight. I understand how you feel about children."

He studied me. I tried to not cover up or appear nervous. It would tip him off more if I tried to hide.

"You're lying." His icy tone sent chills through my body, and panic bubbled in the core of me.

"No... no, I would never..." I stammered, trying to remain calm, but I backed up a few steps.

He launched himself at me. His fists hitting me repeatedly. In my face, my stomach, chest, or anywhere else he could reach. His eyes were flaming. I shut mine, so I didn't look at him while he beat the life out of me, literally. I could almost feel the minute the baby died, or maybe that was me, my heart and soul dying.

Part of me wanted to fight him, to protect myself and the baby. The other part of me knew it would be worse if I didn't just take it and let this happen. He would only get angrier if I fought. I'd made that mistake in the past.

He screamed at me, punching me over and over. Then he did something he had never done. He picked me up and threw me across the room. My head hit the wall, and I saw stars.

He then grabbed me by my neck, picking me up, and pinning me against the wall.

"You are so careless! You are so stupid! Was it your plan to leave me?" He growled and snarled in my face. "You were going to Richmond to have that baby! If you think I will ever let you go, I won't! You are mine, Anna-Rose, don't you ever forget that. You took vows."

He continued his rant while the darkness overtook me. I was thankful for it. If only for a moment of time, I welcomed the escape.

I don't know how long the beating lasted or how long I was unconscious, but I woke to light coming in the window and a silent house. I tried to move and found pain throughout my body. There was blood caked on my face and in my hair, and I knew without looking that it would be pooled at my legs.

I half crawled and half pulled myself down the hallway to the kitchen, then pulled myself up at the sink. I put the stopper in the bottom so it would fill up with water. Slowly, I cleaned myself up with a clean rag.

The water ran red, and soon I had to empty the sink and start the process anew. It was an aching and long process as I winced at every movement.

I then made my way to the outhouse. It was a long, agonizing walk. My eyes darted back and forth, watching for James or even his men. I didn't want them to see me like this. It was heartbreaking to know that I would lose another baby, or that I lost it already. I wasn't sure.

As I finished in the outhouse, I made my way slowly back to the house. I changed to clean clothes. Wincing through the pain, but I didn't want to look in the mirror. I knew what I would find. A face that I no longer recognized, full of cuts and bruises. It would take time to heal physically, but emotionally, I never would.

But seeing the state of my clothing, I knew there was no use trying to save them. I burned it in the fireplace. I would need fabric to make a new dress.

"That one had been my favorite." As I watched it burn, I mumbled.

I then noticed that James has set my trunks on the porch and the wagon was missing. Looking out to the fields, I didn't see anyone. He must have gone into town for the day. Maybe to cash in my ticket. I knew he would never let me leave now.

Looking at the trunks, my heart sunk even more. I would never be free of him. The pain in my chest and sides was so bad as I tried to drag them inside. I collapsed on the porch, crying in pain and heartbreak.

"He is evil." I screamed at the sky. "Why? Oh, why?"

I begged. I pleaded. Looking for an answer to why I had been tied to this evil man. No answer came. No spiritual being spoke.

I was alone.

After I was cried out, I opened each trunk and slowly dragged my things back to the bedroom and put them away. It was a long, painful process as every inch of me throbbed and ached.

With that done, I began prepping for supper. I had no strength to butcher a chicken or rabbit, so I pulled out one of the smoked hams, then peeled potatoes, roasted corn, and got biscuits baked.

When darkness came and no James showed, I paced back and forth, peering out the window every few minutes. Perhaps he wasn't coming back tonight, but I couldn't take a chance on upsetting him if a meal wasn't on the table the minute he came in the door. After an hour of pacing, sitting, and pacing some more. I let the fire dim and I went to bed.

It was a fitful, painful night and when morning dawned, I realized James had not come home. This had never happened before, at least not without warning.

It would leave a shadow over my day. Would he come home, or would he stay gone? I couldn't know. I would have to do my day as if he was coming home.

By the end of the day, there still was no James. I had wasted a day's worth of food, which would now go to the pigs, because I had no appetite.

Every noise had me jumping and flinching. For the second night, I went to bed alone. I had to admit; I liked this part.

Just before I fell asleep, I vowed never to have a baby with this man again. I would get a better mixture to prevent this and I also made a plan that would ensure he never hurt me again. I was done.

Chapter Twenty-Four: Lindsey (July Present Day)

I had just checked in and given my newest guests the tour of the house and property. I was getting better at it. I knew the questions that had been asked with prior guests and had added them to my spiel.

Today's guests were a group of girlfriends away for a trip. It reminded me of my own circle. I missed Simone the most. I hoped she could get away again soon.

A car coming down the road caught my attention. I wasn't expecting any more guests.

"Who the...?"

I peeked out the window. *Oh, that's right.* Jack was bringing my coffee order today.

I stepped outside with my ever-present sidekick, Misty, at my heel, just as he got parked. I waved from the porch.

"Wowee, look what you have done with this place?" He whistled in appreciation as he stepped out, scanning the property.

"Yeah? Thanks. I have worked hard."

"It shows." He pulled a box out of the passenger seat, and then came on to the porch. "Do I get a tour?"

My guests were settling in, and we didn't have a planned activity for an hour. It would be the perfect time to do it.

"Yeah, I've got some time. Follow me. We'll drop that in the kitchen on the way."

We stepped inside and he commented on the foyer as we walked through.

"I'd been here a few times in my teens. You know the stories, right?" I nodded, so he continued. "Kids would sneak over here to mess with the ghost."

"Did you see him?"

"Nah, mostly one idiot would jump out to startle the others." He chuckled. "I was usually *that guy*."

"Ah, I can imagine." I laughed with him. I'd only met him now twice, but he had that class clown vibe about him.

"Yeah, I was *always* that guy." He set the box of coffee on the kitchen island. "Wow, look at what you did in here? This is top-notch."

"Thanks. It was a labor of love."

"Clearly. Business has been good?"

"It has." I smiled with pride. "I can't show you the upstairs as I have guests, but it is a night and day difference."

"Well, based on what I'm seeing downstairs, I can only imagine." He smiled.

"Want to see the backyard?"

"Yep, Marley has been bragging about all the beautiful babies she's sold you. She said you're doing really well with them."

"I'm trying. I've never raised animals alone before. Though I helped my aunt and uncle a few summers, but that was many, many years ago."

We walked to the barnyard where all the animals were. They came running to the fence, clucking, bleating, baying, oinking, and quacking at me.

I greeted them all with head pets and hellos.

"Wowee, this is quite the herd. They all look great." He looked around. "This is an impressive setup. Did you do it yourself?"

"Most of it, yes, but I got some help from Frank and also a little help from Greg and his construction crew."

He turned towards my small garden, which had come in really well. I had already harvested a few veggies.

"That's a gorgeous garden. You did that too?"

I turned to face it as well. It was about a quarter of an acre garden now. I'd started with a quarter of that. Though still small compared to some of the neighboring farms, but for a one-woman show, it was massive.

"Yeah. I've been busy out here."

"I can tell. Must be why we don't see you in town more." He added a wink.

I looked at my animals to avoid him seeing me blush.

"Yeah, I've become a hermit out here." I chuckled lightly. "I need to get out more, I guess."

"How about dinner with me? Tomorrow night?"

"Oh, gosh, that would be nice, but I have guests... I can't–"

"I understand." He frowned and looked down.

"No, I was going to say, not tomorrow, but the next day I can."

"Oh, alrighty, that works." He smiled again. I liked when he smiled. It lit up his entire face. "I can pick you up, at say four? It's a bit of a drive to Waco."

"Waco?"

"Yeah, I'm not taking you to dinner at the Wagon Wheel. I love my grannie and my Aunt Lara, but it's not the best place for a first date."

"Oh, so it's a date." I smirked.

"Yeah, we're both single. Both workaholics, so we deserve a night out."

"Workaholics?"

"Okay, maybe you more than me, but still." He winked. "I need to get goin'. I gotta get back to the shop."

"Who's the workaholic now?"

"Touché!"

We walked around the side of the house rather than go back through it. We paused at his truck; a little electricity sparked between us along with a slightly awkward moment of *where do we go from here*? Or perhaps that was just me.

"Well, I'll see you on Wednesday at 4." He said.

"See ya then."

He hopped in, offered me a salute before backing and then turning down the driveway. I stood there a moment, smiling like an idiot. I had a date.

"Anna-Rose!" the ghostly voice snarled in the wind.

A shiver ran through me, and I turned towards the house. Of course, I saw nothing.

One of my guests stepped out to ask if it was time to feed the animals.

"Yes, I'll meet you around back." I smiled and began walking towards the barn.

I tried to shake off the feeling that I was being watched by an extremely angry ghost. If he really thought I was his wife, he probably didn't like that I'd accepted a date from another man.

"I'm not your wife." I whispered firmly to the air.

There was no reply, so I took his silence as he agreed and I got on with entertaining my guests.

Like all my guests, these loved the animals and wanted to spend as much time playing with them as they could. But soon the animals, still being young, got tired and one by one, they started napping.

This signaled a change in activity, so I served them wine and a charcuterie board full of local cheeses and meats, plus some veggies from my garden and fruits from a neighboring farm.

They giggled and chatted while I went clean up and prep for supper. I smiled as I heard the joyful sounds from inside the kitchen. I loved my job.

Workaholic, ha.

~ ~

Wednesday came. I checked the ladies out.

"We had a blast!" They gushed as I printed receipts. "We will definitely be back."

"Next time, maybe a weekend will be available." One commented.

Her tone had a slight edge to it. I knew weekday trips weren't ideal, but it couldn't be helped. I had no weekends available until early next year.

"Yeah, I'm sorry. It appears I'm popular." I beamed.

"We can see why. This place is amazing." Another said.

"Recommend us to your family and friends." I called as they made their way out and to their waiting car.

They waved and called back that they would. The one adding, "but on a weekend next time."

She would not let that go and it would likely go into her review of the place if she left one. Nothing I could do to control that. I'd let it go, but not going to lie, it stung a bit.

I stood there only a moment, watching the car disappear down the road, and then it turned left to head toward the highway.

"Alright, Misty, let's get these rooms cleaned and ready for tomorrow's guests."

She wagged her tail, and we headed upstairs.

A couple of hours later, I was moving the last set of sheets from the washer to dryer and took the recently dried linens back-up to make the bed. I checked the time. Just an hour until my date, but I still needed to tend to the animals and get a shower.

"Ugh." I needed to get a move on. I smoothed the comforter, plumped a pillow, then hustled out to the barnyard.

The animals were always happy to see me. I filled water troughs, added hay and pellets to their stalls, then threw out mealworms for the chickens in their coop. Once that was done, I got them all into their nighttime enclosures. I wanted to keep everyone safe from predators.

"Okay, I have fifteen minutes to grab a shower and make myself beautiful."

I sprinted inside, got the water going while I stripped and brushed my teeth quickly. Once the water warmed, I hopped in. The new rose scented soap made me linger a bit. I inhaled the scent to relax my nerves, but I had to hurry, so I could only enjoy it for a split second.

I rinsed, then jumped out, drying myself as quickly as I could. Then I twisted my hair up into a loose bun.

"That fixes the hair being wet problem." I said to my reflection.

I put on a touch of mascara and a tinted lip gloss, then threw on a flowy, wine colored sundress with cowboy boots. Checking myself in the full-length mirror, my mind flashed to the pictures of Anna-Rose. While she never wore this type of clothing, the pictures I had seen, her hair was always up in a similar style to this. We were nearly twins.

The sound of a car coming down the driveway caused me to break from my reflection.

"Must be Jack." I said to Misty. "You take care of the house and I'll be back later."

I opened the front door with a smile, just as he knocked on it.

"Hey."

"Hey, yourself. Look at you." He smiled. "You look beautiful."

"Well, thank you. You look nice yourself."

"Are you ready?" He put his arm out, so I hooked mine with his.

"I am."

When we got to his truck, he held his hand for me to climb into it. I thanked him. He jogged around to the driver's side.

"Let's go."

We had a near hour's drive to the restaurant. It wasn't all the way in Waco, just south of it, but still a trek for dinner.

"So, this is a new place. My buddy is actually the owner. Casey's Restaurant and Bar." Jack said.

"Oh, nice."

"Yeah, it's not super fancy or anything, but it is nicer than anything we have in Wisteria. Plus, my dad, aunt, and grannie won't be there watching us." He chuckled.

"That's true." I could only imagine what it was like to date in this small-town where you were related to so many people.

It was slightly awkward driving this far for a date with a man I didn't know well, but we somehow had enough to talk about. The typical likes or dislikes, childhood memories and about our families. I already knew quite a bit about him because June loved to talk when I would go into the diner.

"So, what is it like living in a haunted house? Have you seen the ghost?"

How much should I share? Would he think I was crazy that I'd actually had a few incidents with him? They were terrifying. Nobody would understand those.

"Oh, gosh, yeah, he's a little scary, actually. I've had a few encounters with him."

"Really? I was joking. I thought it was a myth."

"Yeah, I wish. He is always calling for his wife, Anna-Rose."

"Wow. That's crazy." He signaled to exit the freeway. "You know, you look like her."

"You've seen pictures of her?"

"Yeah, they used to have her pictures up in our high school, and I'm sure you've seen the display at the library. She was a big donor to the school or something back in her day, anyway. She's a big part of the history of this town."

I guess I shouldn't be surprised he has seen her picture. I didn't take him as a library guy, but then I didn't know him well either.

"Ah. Yeah, the library was a surprise to see."

"I'm not sure why, only because I didn't know her, but people here loved her. She left quite a legacy."

"It seems so."

I was still reading her journals and had learned a lot about her. She had a heartbreaking marriage. She notes how much abuse she took from him. The most recent entry, she lost another baby at his hand. I cried reading it. Her words were so moving, but also having lost a baby myself, I knew that soul crushing feeling.

"I wish I would have known her. She really seemed like an interesting person." He said as he pulled into a parking spot.

"Me too." I was getting to know her, but reading her journals differed from knowing someone.

As we got out of the truck, I took in the area and the restaurant. It was a large brick and stucco place with a bright blue metal roof. The parking lot was half full at 5:00 p.m.

I guess it wasn't just Wisteria that ate early. Speakers outside were blasting country music. It was a toe-tapping tune, and the closer we got to the front door, you could almost feel the positive vibes coming from inside.

This was going to be fun. I thought as I stole a look at Jack.

He caught me and smiled, then opened the door, and we stepped in. Though it was a large space, the inside was broken up into sections, making each feel more intimate.

To the left, there was a bar area that was through another door, almost separate from the restaurant. We didn't go in that door, but I could see it through a window. It was mostly empty, though it looked like it could be a fun date place.

"Hi, two?" The hostess asked.

"Yes, thank you."

She scanned her list and then grabbed a couple of menus. "Follow me."

Once we were seated, a server came over to take our drink order. We both ordered iced tea. It was a popular choice here, which I learned quickly.

"Great. I'll get these right out and bring you some fresh bread."

We scanned the menu.

"The chicken fried steak here is some of the best in Texas." He offered.

"I was actually eying this redfish."

"Oh, that's good too. Honestly, everything is wonderful. Casey's a talented chef and has hired a wonderful staff."

The server brought our drinks, and we placed our order. We chatted about this or that. Nothing special. Our food arrived. The fish was excellent. Near the end of our meal, Casey came out to say hi.

"This is Lindsey. She bought the Collins' old place." Jack said.

"Oh really. Did you tell her about us all sneaking in there back in the day?" Casey asked.

"I did. She's actually had experience with James Collins."

"Dang, really?"

I didn't really want this to spread too much. It was bad enough that Sunday had indeed put it in the article, but she had spun it, so it was positive. But honestly, how positive could a ghost be?

"I have. He is a tool."

"That's the stories we always heard. Not that we knew anyone who knew him personally." Casey said. "Some of our grandparents and great-grandparents knew Anna-Rose, though."

I nodded. Thankfully, they changed the subject and then he thanked us for coming out. We wrapped up our dinner, then made our way back to Wisteria.

It was dark when we arrived. Misty ran out to greet me.

"Hey, girl."

"She looks so good. Dad would be happy."

I looked at him and smiled as we walked up the few steps to my front door. It felt a little strange to be nearly 40 and going on a first date like this. The awkward goodnight dance of not knowing if I should invite him in or simply say goodbye here.

"I had fun. I hope we can get together again." He said.

"I'd like that."

Tension cracked in the air as we stood there, not moving for a few seconds. He was the one to break it, slowly taking my hand. A warmth spread through me at his simple touch.

"May I kiss you?" He whispered, moving closer to me.

"Yeah."

When our lips touched, there was a heart stopping scream from inside the house. We pulled apart and neither of us moved for what felt like an eternity. My body went ice cold as the blood rushed out of me.

"Was that him?"

"It sounds like it. I'm in for an active night tonight."

He looked around with wide eyes, and his breathing seemed to quicken. I understood, even though I was sort of getting used to him, the ghost always caused me to tremble. I squeezed his hand.

He looked at me, "Not suggesting anything happen with us, but do you want me to stay? I can sleep on the couch."

For a moment, I seriously considered it. It would be nice not to be alone with the ghost tonight because I had a feeling, he was going to be pissed that Anna-Rose went out on a date. Even though I wasn't her, he thought I was.

"I can't ask that of you. Plus, he seems to be scared of Misty. Since getting her, he seems to not mess with me as much." Though he still did some.

"Well, alright." His voiced wavered as he studied the house and then to me. "If you're sure, I will leave you to it."

He leaned forward, giving me a quick kiss and then skipped down the steps. Waving as he drove away. His truck hesitated at the end of the drive before he turned right toward town.

"That didn't end the way it should have."

I could have sworn there was an evil laugh in the air.

"Screw you, James Collins!"

Chapter Twenty-Five: Lindsey (July Present Day)

The night of my date with Jack had really set James Collins on edge. He had been louder than usual. His screams and rants could be heard all night, but thankfully, he mostly left me alone. I credit Misty for keeping him at bay.

By morning, I was more tired than when I went to sleep, but I had guests arriving today and I needed to finish getting the last bed made.

I stretched and looked at my dog. She yawned from her place on my bed, but didn't make a move to get up.

"We need coffee. Lots of coffee."

She still didn't move, but instead snuggled further into the blankets.

"Fine, stay here. I'll do everything."

I chuckled as I made my way to the bathroom and then straight for the coffeepot. When I didn't have guests, I didn't make a full pot. I used my coffee press when it was just me.

The water was heating in my electronic kettle while I measured out a few tablespoons of Jack's coffee beans. The strong smell waking me a bit. Once the water was ready, I poured it over, stirred, and then waited.

While that brewed, I peeked out the window. It was raining, but the sun wasn't up yet so I couldn't see the rain well. That would make feeding the animals more difficult, but they loved the rain, especially the pigs.

I then dropped a couple of pieces of bread in the toaster. While the bread toasted, I grabbed some of the fresh fruit I always had on hand.

Once my simple breakfast was ready, I took my toast, fruit, and coffee to the back porch. It was covered from the rain, and I could listen to the country come alive as the sun tried to come up. The clouds blocked it, but the sky brightened slightly as the sun fought for its turn to shine.

Mornings here were my favorite. Usually, the ghost didn't bother me and I could sit for a moment, reflecting.

My date had gone well, but being interrupted by a spirit tantrum was not the ending I'd hoped for. I would have liked to have a lingering goodnight kiss and then a beautiful, swoony moment when I close the door behind me and giggle with glee about the cute guy I'd just been out with.

I didn't get that. Instead, I got a jealous ghost. The fog came flying down the stairs the moment I came in the door. It was all around me.

"Who was that? Why were you with another man?" He screamed over and over. "You're my wife!"

I tried fighting it, but I couldn't move or speak. It was suffocating. Misty barked until he finally disappeared. He then stomped around all night, but never came near me again.

I wasn't as afraid of him this time; I was more angry. He ruined what should have been a wonderful night. I should have laid in my bed daydreaming about the guy who smelled like coffee and vanilla.

I knew the source of the coffee smell, but I wondered if he got his soap from Suds and Soaps, too. I had recently switched from the vanilla to the rose scented, so at least we didn't smell the same. That thought made me laugh.

The only low point of our date was when our conversation had turned to the ghost. He had asked about James and even told his buddy about it. I didn't know if I wanted everyone to know about my eerie experience, but of course, anyone who read the Wisteria Word knew about it.

It was embarrassing, but really every time I went into town, people asked me about living in the haunted house. They'd tell me I was brave for living here.

I don't know about brave. Though I wasn't sure how I would describe myself. I'd been in a bad situation, and I fixed it. What's that called?

"I don't know, Misty, but brave is not a word I'd use."

She had finally gotten out of bed and had joined me on the porch. At my statement, she simply wagged her tail and then looked out into the yard. She seemed to enjoy our quiet mornings, too.

I finished my breakfast, then took my dishes inside. I put my coffee mug next to the pot and then rinsed my plate. It was still raining, so I grabbed my raincoat and boots and made my way out to the barn.

As I was walking through the rain, the murder of crows came back. They filled the trees and cawed as I made my way to the barn. I looked up just before I went inside. The number of them caused a shiver through my body. I swear one of them was looking me dead in my eyes.

"What?"

It cawed and then flew off.

As a shiver traveled my spine. I shook off the eerie encounter and turned my attention to the happy, familiar sounds, along with ear flicks and wagging tails of my babies greeting me. They turned my mood around quickly, as they all paced around, pushing and pawing at the gates asking to get out.

"Do y'all want to go out in the rain?" It was mid-July, so warm enough for them to be out. "Okay. If y'all insist."

I opened their stalls and then pushed open the door that led to the large, fenced yard. They all waddled and ran out, except for the donkeys who stayed behind. They didn't care for the rain as much. Instead, they stood in the doorway, watching the others.

I got to work cleaning up the stalls, adding fresh water, bedding, and food. The feed and hay were getting low, so I'd need to make a run to the feed store soon.

Once that was done, the rain was letting up, so I walked to the yard. The goats were bouncing and jumping around. The pigs were chasing after the goats and the donkeys remained in the doorway.

A quick visual check. Everyone looked happy and healthy.

Next, I went over to the chicken and duck coops. They were side-by-side and connected to the main barn yard. When I opened the doors, they ran out to join the other babies in the yard.

I watched for only a second or two before turning to clean up their home. I made quick work out of it, then walked to the fence to watch all the animals enjoying a new day.

By the time I was finished, the rain had nearly stopped, so the donkeys had finally joined the fun. I watched them for only a few minutes more because I had to finish prepping for my guests.

My phone chimed. It was Jack wishing me a good morning. *That's a nice surprise.* I thought.

I replied in kind and then hustled to the house to get the final touches done before my guests arrived. I had set the check in at noon each day, which gave me time to do my chores and to get any final prep complete.

The texting continued off and on for the morning, but then we both had to get to work. My guests arrived in a flurry of bags and giggles. It was another girl's trip that once again had me missing my crew.

These always had me missing my friends, which reminded me I would need to call Simone soon to tell her about Jack.

I gave them a quick tour and handed them the schedule.

"I'll be in the kitchen putting together an afternoon snack. You can come out to the back porch whenever you are ready."

"Thank you!" They gushed and giggled as they dropped bags and bounced on beds.

Misty followed me downstairs. She enjoyed having guests, but also stuck close to me. It was like she knew she had to protect me from the spirit, or maybe that was just what I thought.

I headed to the kitchen to cut up fruit and vegetables. I added them to a beautiful, vintage tray that I'd gotten at a rummage sale. It was made of tin and had hand-painted pears on it. I wrapped the tray with plastic wrap to protect it from the foods.

I added a tiny mason jar that was filled with toothpicks. My idea was for them to spear the fruit and veggies with the toothpicks. The final touch was two kinds of dip. A sweet one for the fruit and a tangy one for the veggies.

I set those on the back porch and then brought out a large pitcher of iced tea. I put out mason jar glasses and floral printed dessert plates.

"Oh, napkins!" I ran back in and right into an angry fog.

He yelled, grabbing my arms shaking me. As illogical as it sounded, I could feel myself shaking, even though I know he couldn't hurt me, or I didn't think he could.

Despite that, I let out a blood-curdling scream. Misty came running, barking, and snapping at the fog.

"Stop talking to that man." He demanded.

I tried to speak, to argue with him, but I couldn't. My body was paralyzed. The ladies came running, just as the fog lifted.

"Are you okay?" One asked, putting her arms around me.

"What was that?" Another asked, as she fanned the air.

I tried to catch my breath. He really caught me off guard this time. He usually left me alone during the day.

"You probably won't believe me if I told you." I tried to joke, but my heart was beating so fast, I think it came out with more panic than I meant.

"Well, I think we can figure out it was some kinda evil spirit." The last one crossed her arms and looked around wide-eyed.

"That's the rumor. He usually only messes with me, so y'all don't have to worry."

But if he kept this up, I was going to burn this place to the ground. Maybe I could rebuild on the other side of the property or something.

My biggest concern at the moment was if my guests left and then gave me a bad review online. If they did, it wasn't fair because it wasn't like I invited the ghost here.

"I'm sorry for the trouble." I took a deep breath. I looked at them for reassurance.

"It's okay. We're here to escape reality. What is more of an escape than a haunted house? It will be fun." One friend giggled. Her name was Lacy.

"I agree with Lacy. We're here for fun and that's what we are going to do." Bridget shouted, adding a woot, woot at the end.

"Well, I'm not as happy about it as you two, but I'm in." Jenn added.

"Alright. To start, I put out snacks on the back porch. Let me just grab the napkins."

While the ladies were making their way outside, I retrieved the napkins. I glanced around to make sure I didn't get ambushed by the James fog again.

They were laughing and chatting with each other, seemingly unbothered by the ghost. Relief flooding my body as I realized they were okay with the unwanted resident. I really needed to figure out how to get rid of him.

Perhaps if I kept reading Anna-Rose's journals, something would come to me.

Chapter Twenty-Six: Anna-Rose (1883)

It had been a month since James last beat me. He had disappeared for nearly two weeks.

For the first few days, I lived on edge, not knowing when he would be back or how to live my life that whole week. I wasted more food than I wanted to admit. The pigs were thankful and would be nice and fat when the Fall came.

As the week dragged on with no word or sign of him, I started to not care if he came home at all. I did what I wanted. Plus, I was in too much pain to worry about making him meals he wasn't here to eat. I spent the last few days mostly sleeping. If he came home and found me that way, so be it. I had nothing left to lose.

When he came home, he didn't say a word about where he had been and didn't ask how I was feeling. I didn't expect him to ask, and I would not be honest if he did ask. It would simply upset him, and my body couldn't take anything else.

While he was gone, I had gotten foxglove, which was used to prevent pregnancy and was supposed to be better than the last potion I had. I would not go through that again.

I went about my daily chores with no emotion and not taking in the beauty any longer. He had removed all the color from my world.

I was making the mid-day meal of beef stew for him and the ranch hands, who had all returned when he did. They didn't say a word to me about where they had been or how they knew to come back. It didn't matter. Nothing mattered.

I was shaken from my thoughts at the sound of the men coming in from the fields. They were laughing as they cleaned up at the outside water pump.

I hurriedly got their food plated and set on the table as they came in the door. I smiled absently and out of habit. No sense upsetting the neutral life we were currently living.

"Thanks. Mrs. Collins." the men said as they settled into eat.

James looked up and mumbled his thanks, too. I'm sure it was out of obligation. I didn't reply, just smiled back and pushed my food around in my bowl. Food had no flavor for me anymore, so I barely ate these days, but I served myself a small portion, so it didn't raise any eyebrows.

The meal was quiet except for the sounds of forks scrapping on bowls and the chewing of the men. It was no matter that they didn't speak more to me and didn't even seem to notice I wasn't eating.

The past year, my world had become small and quieter. I only saw my friends at church now, which I had missed more than attend. I rarely attended the after church socials any longer. I once enjoyed those.

When home, I rarely spoke. I had nothing to say, and with only James as company; it offered few opportunities to speak.

As the men finished; I offered more, and then one by one they finished and headed back out. Before James followed them, he looked at me with a look I couldn't read.

He then closed the distance between us, taking me in his arms to kiss me. I let him and didn't fight. I know this meant he was feeling guilty about mistreating me.

"Thank you. Food was good." He said, kissing me once more, before releasing me and then following his men back out to the cattle.

I honestly did not know what they did out there all day, but it kept him out of my hair. For that, I was ever thankful.

I cleaned up from the meal, then went to work in the garden. It was nearly time to rotate crops again. I harvested anything that was ready. Tomorrow I would start getting it prepared for the next plants.

The rest of my day was mundane and typical. It was at our evening meal when things got uncomfortable.

James came in humming a tune, swinging me around in a waltz.

"I'm happy, Anna-Rose. Are you?"

I didn't, couldn't answer that truthfully. I simply smiled.

"Does that mean you are?"

"James, I'm not unhappy."

I didn't know how to answer without getting back handed. It was partially true because I was numb, so I wasn't feeling much of anything.

"I understand that I'm difficult to live with." He pulled me to him. "Perhaps we should try for a baby."

His words felt like a gut punch. I had no plan to bring a life into this world with him in it. I would continue to take the foxglove and hope for the best.

"Okay." I lied.

"Let us start now." He pulled me toward the bedroom.

~ ~

Days later, I was sitting in church waiting for the sermon to start. I had my bible open, reading a few of my favorite verses.

Leonora came in, wrangling her boys into the pew.

"Morning, Anna-Rose." She smiled. Her stomach growing by the day. I laid my hand absently on my empty one.

"Morning, Leonora, boys."

They smiled.

"How ya feelin' these days?" I asked her.

"Big. Ready." She weakly smiled at me, looking only briefly at my stomach. "I'm sorry."

"No, it's fine." I smiled and reached for her hand, giving in a slight squeeze. "I'm happy for you."

Everyone in town knew that James beat me and knew I had lost babies. It was becoming hard to hold my head when I went to town, though I tried.

The pastor walked to the pulpit, cleared his throat, and the room went silent.

"Welcome this beautiful Sunday that God has given us..." He started most of his sermons the same. It was after that when he started preaching about murder.

"Looking to the sixth commandment, it states 'Thou Shalt not Kill'. Now this is not simply the act of killing, no. Murder is far more complex. Think of war. Is it wrong to kill in his case? Maybe, maybe not. That will be for God to decide. Murder is defined by intention and premeditation to kill another person..." He continued.

My mind went to James. He had intentionally killed those innocent babies. Lives we created. That was murder. I knew it was, but hearing it out loud confirmed it in my mind, not just my heart.

But what's worse is now, out of guilt, he has asked us to try for a baby. The loss had hurt me deeply. Asking to create more was a knife in the back.

I was numb through the entire sermon, only hearing the first part. Leonora looked at me a few times and squirmed in her seat. I wonder if she thought about my babies, too.

I couldn't make eye contact. I just kept my eyes straight forward, trying to keep a relaxed face. Nothing to worry about, simply a wife and woman listening to the Sunday Sermon, like I have most Sundays since I moved here.

An hour later, the hymns were sung, and the prayers said, we all filed out. Today there was no picnic or fellowship after, but I wouldn't have stayed, anyway. So, I began the slow walk home, and I had time to reflect on my life.

I was not happy. I was not fulfilled.

Though I didn't know what I should do about it. Was this to be my life from now until I die?

On the way, I found my favorite blackberries were ready to be picked. I removed my bonnet and picked until it was full.

"I'll make a nice pie with these." It brought me a bit of joy. I ate a few on the way home. They were sweet and sour at the same time. It was a small joy.

I got home and immediately got to work on our mid-day meal. It would be smoked ham, fried potatoes with cornbread. Something simple.

"I found blackberries on the way home. I'll make us a nice pie for later." I said to James.

He grumbled something over the book he was reading. I stared at him with disgust as the pastor's words ran through my head. All joy over finding the blackberries disappeared.

I stared at him for a moment, thinking about his intention. His words as he beat me all those times. It was control over me. Control over my life and wanted me all to himself.

I knew I had made the choice to be his wife and our vows said until death parts us. My intention was to fulfill those vows. It was going to be a long, sad life, but I had made my decision.

Sighing quietly, I finished getting our meal together and called him to the table. He came without a word. Like most of our meals, I sat quietly picking at my food, forcing myself to eat something, and serving him as he demanded.

This was my life. I had to accept it.

Chapter Twenty-Seven: Lindsey (July Present Day)

James had been quiet for the rest of those ladies' visit. I had no idea why he came and went. He was so unpredictable. I really needed to research how to get rid of him, but I had non-stop guests and an entire farm to run. It left little time for much else.

Plus, I had started dating, though casually. Currently, it was only texting and chatting when we could, as we both had businesses to run, but we had plans to go out again soon.

Today, I was waiting for my next guests. Checking the time, it was still two hours until they should arrive. I had everything ready for them. Beds made? Check. Towels and bathrooms ready? Check. Schedule of activities has been printed and all the grocery shopping done.

I pulled out my phone to search for *how to get rid of a spirit.*

Pages of articles and videos popped. I skimmed through a few.

"Cleanse the house? Meh." I read on. "Oh, this might work."

It said to uninvited the ghost from the house. Not that I had invited him, exactly. He just came with the house. So how do I uninvite him? I guess I could find a psychic medium to speak to him. That is something I would keep in mind.

I read through a few more articles, but for now my best choice was to ask him to leave. Maybe make things a bit more uncomfortable for him.

Which gave me an idea? He didn't like Misty. Maybe I should get a second dog.

I shot off a text to Jack.

Does your dad have any stray dogs right now?

It was a few minutes before he replied.

Yep. You want another?

Thinking about it

I'll ask him and get back to you

Thanks

With that handled, I made a fresh batch of cookies. It would make the house smell wonderful when the guests arrived. Plus, they had children. They could enjoy them as part of the afternoon snack with lemonade. I had these planned for tomorrow's snack, but I could switch things up to deal with my nervous energy.

I got busy mixing the chocolate chip cookies, adding extra chips. My phone signaled a message as I put the cookies in the oven.

Drying my hands quickly, I picked up my phone to read Jack's reply.

Dad has two right now. Both fixed. Want me to bring them by for you?

That would be awesome. I have guests arriving soon, though.

Let me know. I can bring them after work.

Thanks

That was as easy as the first time. I thought.

But when you knew the local animal rescuer, it was an easy task. I pulled out the cookies and got them cooling.

Misty came in from outside.

"Hey, girl, do you want a doggy friend?"

She wagged her tail and plopped down at my feet.

"That's your answer to everything, but I'll take it as a yes for now."

I cleaned up the cookie mess, then waited for my guests to arrive.

Hours later, my guests arrived were settled in and enjoying time on the back porch with the afternoon refreshments. It was sisters and their families; I smiled as I stood at the sink. It really was the best sound, hearing the laughs and love of the family and friends sharing some downtime.

This was the dream.

My phone chimed.

Is now good?

I looked out at the families before replying.

Yes. Now works

On our way

I stepped on to the porch.

"How's it going?" I asked.

They all looked at me with blissful smiles.

"We're good. This is gorgeous." The one sister said for the group as she gestured out at the property. The rest of them nodded.

"Wonderful." I looked around, unsure how to ask them or tell them that Jack was bringing a couple of dogs for me to see. "Um, so I have a friend coming to bring a couple of dogs, so I will be out front for a few minutes or so. There are board games and cards in that cabinet there and then, when I'm done, we can go to the barnyard to start the animal feedings."

"Mommy, can we see the dogs?" One kid asked. I think her name was Nora.

They all looked at me for the answer.

"Um, yeah, I guess. I just didn't think y'all would want to."

"I love dogs." The little boy, River said. He jumped up and did a little happy dance.

"Well, okay. He should be here any minute with them."

"Are you getting a new dog?" Nora asked as she gave Misty a piece of cookie.

Her mom fussed at her for feeding the dog. Nora's eyes darted to me. I smiled at her, and she returned the smile.

"I'm thinking about it."

"We have two dogs at home. They have fun together." Nora said.

I heard the familiar crush of the gravel road signaling that Jack was here. Then I heard the dogs barking.

"Sounds like they're here." I nodded my head for them to follow me.

The kids jumped up and followed me. Nora took my hand as we walked around. I had little experience with children, even though I wanted kids, so this was a new but pleasant surprise.

"Hey, there." Jack called out as he got out of the truck. The passenger door opened and out hopped Bart.

"Oh, hey, Bart. I didn't know you were coming too. Nice to see you."

"I wouldn't miss a chance to say hi and see Misty, too."

I greeted both men with a quick hug.

"These are my new friends, Nora, River, and that is... um, Gage, right?" The quietest one nodded his head. I smiled at him. I didn't introduce the parents that were looking on. This was about the kids and a dog. "They wanted to help pick out my dog."

Misty was sniffing around and whining. She stood against the truck trying to see in the back. Jack scratched her head.

"Are you ready for a friend?" He said to the dog. "She looks great, Lindsey. I knew you were the right person for her."

"She's been a wonderful dog." I didn't mention about her helping against James Collins.

I recently read an entry in Anna-Rose's diary that said he doesn't like dogs, which was another reason I wanted another dog. It seemed to be a key to keeping him under control.

I walked to the back of the truck and peeked in the back. They had two large kennels with three dogs in total. One looked like it was one of Misty's pups.

"I know you didn't want a puppy before, but that's the last of Misty's babies, and I thought maybe you would want him. He is nearly five months old now and is ready to be neutered. I have the appointment set for next month. He'll be almost six months by then."

That's why Misty was trying to get into the truck.

"Can I see?" Nora asked.

"Sure. Let me get them all out," Jack said, dropping the tailgate and then opening the latches on the kennels.

Misty was right there waiting for the dogs to come out. I thought she was going to wag herself in half. When her golden colored baby came to the edge of the truck bed, she stood and licked his face. He whimpered and wagged his tail.

I picked him up. He licked my face.

"Well, aren't you sweet," Misty was trying to smell him. "Here's mom."

I set him down, and they greeted each other with whimpers, licks, head to tail smelling. The other two dogs smelled her too, but then greeted the kids and ran around us, pouncing on each other.

"Wow, how will I decide?" I laughed. "Did you name any of them yet?"

"Um, just that one there. I've been calling him Rocky. The other two just have more like nicknames. Misty's pup, I've just been calling Big Guy. He was the largest of her litter. Then the last one there, just calling him dog. Not really a name."

"Alright." That didn't make the decision easier, but watching Misty and Big Guy together, I was really leaning towards taking him.

The kids were running around with all four of the dogs. They all seemed good with children, which was important because I had a lot of families here. All four seemed to be friendly with each other as well. This was going to be a tough decision.

Nora came over while I was watching them all play.

"Ms. Lindsey, I think you should get her baby. She's a good mommy."

I turned to watch Misty and Big Guy playing together. She was gentle and kissing him. She seemed happy to have one of her babies.

"I think you're right." I smiled down at my new little friend. "What do you think I should call him?"

"Oh," she clapped her hands. "What about... Sully? Like the monster in the movie!"

"Sully, huh?" It didn't seem to fit him. I would need to think about it. "Maybe. Do you have another ideas?"

"If you don't like that, what about Scooby? Or Mikey or Mickey?" Nora was trying.

"What about Tucker?" I suggested.

"Who is Tucker?" She was clearly wanting something she was familiar with and could relate to. I could understand that.

"I *think* he is going to be my new dog." I smiled.

She giggled and ran to him, yelling Tucker. He turned toward her with a wagging tail and a small yip. Tucker it is.

Jack and Bart were simply watching with broad smiles. They nodded when they realized I was taking the puppy. Bart let out a whistle which signaled all four dogs to run to him.

"Well, I'll take these two back, unless you think you want more than just two dogs?" Bart asked hopefully.

"It's really tempting, but I think for now, just one more. I'm sure you will find them both good homes."

"I always manage." He reached into the back, pulling out a collar and leash, handing it to me. "I'll call the vet's office later and have them switch Tucker to you." He added with a wink. "I like the name."

"I'll call you later." Jack said as they got the other two dogs loaded.

"Sounds good." I smiled at him.

With the help of their parents, I made sure the kids and my two dogs were back, and we watched as Jack and Bart drove on down the road. Jack waved his hand out the window just before he turned right to head to town. Tucker came over, plopping on my feet.

Glad to have that done, I checked the time.

"Who wants to feed some farm animals now?" I turned toward my guests.

Everyone cheered, then followed me around to the back of the house. I grabbed some of the small cups that I filled with pellets. Most of the animals could and would eat these, and it was easy for the kids to handle, even the smallest ones.

I gave them a quick lesson on the various animals, including their names. They all knew so much already, which made my job easier and more fun.

"If you want to brush them, which they all love, I have some brushes over there."

The kids giggled and started throwing food for the animals. The goats trotted around, jumping on their various play structures, and twitching their cute tails.

The pigs followed me around, but if food fell near them, they would gobble it up. The donkeys took to Gage, maybe because they had got his bucket away from him and had gotten to eat all the pellets.

He giggled, but his wide eyes told a different story.

Even the parents were getting into the fun. One mom grabbed a brush, then sat on the bench I had in the yard. That's when Goat Paige climbed right into her lap. She laughed and looked at her husband. He snapped a few pictures.

I stepped out and leaned on the fence to watch.

That's when an icy chill ran through me. It was James. I just knew it.

"You will never be rid of me." The wind whispered.

Chapter Twenty-Eight: Lindsey (July Present Day)

I swiped on a bit of mascara and lip gloss, then smoothed my blouse.

"What do y'all think?" I turned toward my dogs.

They wagged their tails at me. Tucker had settled in well with us. It was as if he had always been a part of our family, even though it had only been a few days.

"Well, thank you." I said to them. "I'll take it you approve."

They wagged their tails again.

I was getting ready for a date with Jack. We had finally matched our schedules again.

We were heading to a music festival in a neighboring town. It was another small-town but larger than Wisteria at nearly 10,000 people. The shops and restaurants stayed open longer, and even better, his family wouldn't be around.

Knowing I would be away for the evening, I'd already taken care of all the animals, so there was nothing left to do but wait for Jack to arrive.

While I waited, I pulled up my bookings on my computer, just to review what I had for tomorrow. I was always one to be prepared; I liked to memorize the schedule, at least the best I could.

The familiar crush of gravel signaled a smile on my face and butterflies in my stomach. Misty and Tucker started getting excited, bouncing up and down with full body wiggles. They both loved people.

I opened the door as Jack was stepping out of the truck. His smile sent goosebumps and curled my toes.

"Wowee, look at you. Beautiful." He stepped forward to kiss my check, then greeted each dog.

"Well, thank you." I smiled. "Alright, doggies, stay. I'll be back."

"You talk to them like they are people." He chuckled. "My dad does too."

"They are people. Sort of."

He laughed, then opened the truck door for me, helping me in. While he jogged around to the driver's side, I peeked out the window to ensure the dogs stayed back. They learned quickly and were obedient. Tucker mostly followed in his mom's lead.

"Ready?" He smiled.

"Ready."

He backed up, taking a left at the end of my driveway. This would take us to the freeway and then we would head west for about fifteen miles to Acreview.

"They have a musical festival every year. It is usually pretty good. Local bands from all around perform."

"It sounds fun. I can't wait."

I had looked it up and saw pictures from the previous festival. They had food vendors, local farmers, and artists with their products, and then, of course, the musicians.

"So, how's things with the ghost?"

"He's been... quieter." I frowned.

"That's good, right? You make it sound like that's a bad thing."

"He seems to get quiet right before he... isn't."

I couldn't be so lucky that he had gone away when I got Tucker, though that had been my hope. Even if he had gone because of the two dogs, I knew I wouldn't be able to fully relax. I'd always be waiting for him to show again.

"What are you going to do?"

"I honestly don't know, but so far it hasn't hurt my business, so I'm okay."

"Well, that's good. By the way, that was a nice piece that Sunday ran in the paper."

"Yeah, it turned out well." It had also gotten me a few more bookings. "I hadn't realized they had such an online following, not just locals."

"I think it's Sunday's writing style. She has a way with words."

"She does. She made me sound far more interesting than I am."

"Oh, you are very interesting even without her wordsmithing." He grinned.

"Well, thank you."

Arriving in Acreview, we were greeted by crowds of people, orange traffic signs directing us to various parking lots, and the sounds of rock music. We followed the line of other festival goers and then were waved into a spot by a parking attendant.

We hopped out of the truck, and he grabbed my hand, squeezing it slightly as he smiled. As we weaved our way through to the town square, the music got louder and the crowds thicker.

"This is something." I yelled above the crowd, noise, and music. The drumbeat was thumbing in the air.

"Yeah, fun, right?"

I nodded because the closer I moved to the music, the louder it got, and speaking was going to be near impossible. He gestured if I wanted a drink. I nodded again, so he gave me the be right back sign. I found a batch of ground to sit on as I listened to the current rock band and waited for him to return.

After several minutes, he found me. He passed me a beer and then took a seat next to me on the ground. We listened to the band and sipped at our beers; conversation was completely impossible.

"Thank you, Acreview! We are the Southern Three. Hope you've enjoyed our set. Next up, the Stevens band."

There was a lull in the music while the bands changed. The crowd shifted as some of the audience moved on, and others came to join.

"Wanna stay or walk around?"

"Let's have a look around."

I was curious to see what the locals offered. Maybe there were products I could add to my bed-and-breakfast.

He held his hand out to help me off the ground, and then we made our way to the booths. They had everything from jewelry to vegetables and everything in between. I stopped in front of a wind chime booth. The tinkling sound caught my attention.

"Wow. These are beautiful."

"They are." Jack examined one.

"These are all handmade." A gentleman with kind eyes and wisdom etched on his face smiled with pride. "I hand hammer them for the perfect sound."

"They're amazing." I flipped the price tag over on one. Not bad. "This one is $65, correct?"

"That's right."

"I'll take it. PayPal?"

"Yes. You can find the address right on that sign." He pointed to the sign on this table as he took it down and grabbed a box from behind him. He laid the chimes gingerly inside and wrapped tissue around it. While he did that, I paid via the app, sending it to his address.

He verified and then handed me the wrapped box. "Thank you so much."

"Thank you, Sam."

He smiled as we turned away from the booth.

"Where are you going to put it?" Jack said.

"I know just the place. Right off the back porch."

We visited several other booths. I bought some soaps, a handmade candle, and gathered a lot of business cards.

Jack ran into a few people he knew and introduced me.

"Oh, you opened that new bed-and-breakfast everyone is raving about." A friend he introduced as George.

"I don't know about raving about, but yep, that's me."

"Have you had an experience with that ghost?" George asked.

"Um, a little."

I was starting to hate this question. It was the first thing everyone asked when they found out where I lived. I needed to get used to it; I supposed.

"When we ended our last date, he interrupted things." Jack chuckled.

"Really? Wow." George said. "Remember when we'd sneak over there? We always scared the bejeebies out of the others."

"Yeah, good times." Jack laughed.

We said goodbye to him and then headed for the food tent. They had a large tent set up with picnic tables set up row after row. It was just grab a spot that looked good and get to know your neighbors.

We stood near the many food trucks and booths set up around the tent.

"What're you feeling?" He asked as we scanned the many options.

"Barbecue?"

"Sounds good to me."

We got in the long line. The length of the line suggested it was a popular choice. We talked casually about the bands we'd seen and the great shopping we'd done.

"I think I'm going to get a few paintings from Iris. Those landscapes really capture the hills and colors." I said.

"She's talented. I think she might have gone to school with my mother." He looked over his shoulder at her booth. "Those would look great in your house."

We finally made it to the front of the line, placed our order for a couple of barbecue beef sandwiches, fries, and a bottle of water, then stepped to the side to wait.

When our food was ready, we gathered it along with a stack of napkins.

"There're a few spots over there." I nodded.

We made our way to the empty table.

"Are these available?" Jack asked.

"All yours, bud." The older gentleman said. He had on a Texas A&M Polo shirt. "As long as y'all are Aggies fans?"

I honestly didn't have a team, so I smiled. "Of course we are."

Though I wasn't sure what side Jack was on. He simply winked at me.

"They had some season last year. I couldn't believe that bowl game," Jack said.

"That game. I thought for sure I'd have a heartache." He continued to talk to Jack about all things Aggie related. It gave me time to take in the surroundings.

I felt made for this small-town life. Everyone was welcoming and friendly. They were quick with a smile or a hello. I had so many offer me help or been a resource when needed.

Plus, I enjoyed times like this when it seemed the whole town, and those around it, came together to enjoy a beautiful day with each other around good food and music.

I watched all the happy families, laughing together, sharing a meal. Little ones running around or dancing to the music.

There was that familiar ache deep inside. A child was the only thing really missing from my life. Well, a husband, a partner, was also missing if I went a traditional route. Obviously, there were other options.

I let my eyes dart sideways to take in Jack as I continued to talk to the friendly older man. He had introduced himself as Merv.

Jack was a few years older. Married once, like me. They didn't have children either, but that was because she had been finishing college and he was working. Once she was done with her degree, she threw herself into her job and, in his words; they were working on building careers.

He had said that over time; they grew apart. Jobs, projects, and the stress of building their careers.

"There were no hard feelings exactly, but when she started dating someone, I had to get out of there. That's how I ended up back here." He had shared during a late-night phone call.

"Better than my marriage. I was laid off and came home to find my husband, now-ex, in the middle of packing up to leave me."

"Oh, wow, that's... awful. I'm sorry."

"Thanks. I'm much happier now, and realized he was right. We had grown apart as well."

He caught me looking at him now and grinned. "Penny for your thoughts?"

"Just thinking about how great today has been."

He squeezed my thigh lightly. "It has been nice."

We wrapped up our lunch, then finished at the festival before heading back to my house. I watched the beautiful scenery as we drove. Farms with neat rows of crops, corrals with various animals grazing. It was mesmerizing.

He finally signaled to turn down my driveway. When my house came into view, it took my breath away as it always did. It was beautiful. I felt true peace.

"I had fun," he said, putting the truck in park.

"I did too. I'm glad we could finally make this happen."

"Me too." He leaned over.

When our lips touch, I swear my toes curled. I reached my hand up to grab his arm, pulling him closer. It felt like forever since I'd really been kissed.

"Wanna come in?" I whispered.

"Sure."

We hopped out of the truck. The dogs were waiting on the porch.

"Hey, babies." I scratched them both behind the ears, then unlocked the front door.

Jack greeted the dogs as we made our way inside and to the living room. I flipped on a lamp, leaving the house somewhat dark with only some dim light coming from the setting sun. He pulled me to him.

"Hi." He whispered.

"Hi."

Our lips met. The kiss started soft and slow, but grew to a crushing passion. We made our way to the couch, falling into each other. His arms felt strong and warm around me.

It had been so long since I'd made out with a man. His lips were soft yet firm, his tongue licked slightly at my lips. My stomach fluttered as the kiss turned into me, removing my shirt and pulling at his, when I heard it.

My heart leaped into my throat as the sound of loud, angry footsteps started down the hallway.

"Anna-Rose, I warned you!"

We looked up as the fog engulfed us. I couldn't see Jack even though his face had split seconds ago been touching mine. Though I heard a strangled sound come from his general direction. I was frozen in place, every muscle in my body throbbed and pulsed.

"Anna-Rose, you are married to me!"

The shouts came with suffocating force. I gasped and choked as the cold squeezed all around.

"You **will** obey me."

Another strange sound came from Jack's side, but I still couldn't see him and didn't even know if he was actually there. I tried in vain to reach my hand out to him, but I couldn't move.

That's when I finally heard the familiar sounds of Misty and Tucker. They were growling and barking. The ghost cursed, squeezed me once more, throwing me back hard against the couch as it dissipated. I felt my nose running.

When I reached up, I realized I had a nosebleed. *Crap.* This was new.

I looked over to see Jack, wide-eyed, gasping. He looked over at me as his vision seemed to clear.

"Whoa." He finally said, jumping to his feet so quickly. It was as if he had sat on something sharp.

"I... I'm sorry."

I stood, scanning for a tissue or something to stop the blood. I ran to the kitchen quickly and back. As I tried desperately to stop the bleeding, I held a bunch of tissues against my nose.

He was still standing there bug eyed, shaking, and speechless.

"Are you okay?" Even though this one was extremely violent, I recovered more quickly than Jack had.

"I... I gotta go."

He bolted before giving me a chance to talk to him and didn't even look back. I ran to the door, trying to catch up, but all I saw were taillights.

"Damn you, James Collins! I am not your wife."

I swear I heard laughter as my tears fell. One of the best dates I'd been on with a wonderful guy had ended badly, violently, and he would likely never speak to me again.

I wish he would have stayed to talk it out with me at least, but I don't blame him for running. It was an intense experience.

But, gosh darn, I was mad.

Chapter Twenty-Nine: Lindsey (August Present Day)

It had been a week since my date with Jack. He had called the next day, ending things between us.

"That scared me like I have never been scared." He started. "I'm man enough to admit that I can't compete with a mad ghost."

"Jack..." I started to argue, but realized there was no point. "I'm sorry. I am really sorry."

"How can you live with him?" When just the day before, he had been interested and intrigued by the ghost, now his tone was terror and disgust.

"I honestly don't know."

We ended the call after that with just a few kind words. I'm sure before long word would get around town about how violent my house mate was. The thing is, I didn't want him here either. He was the throned bush in my otherwise lush garden life.

"Damn it." I cursed under my breath.

But then I got a call from Simone an hour later. My life felt a little more hopeful again.

"I saw you had availability at your house this week, so guess who booked your last two spots?" She asked.

"If it isn't you, this is a cruel joke."

"Yep, it's me. Your girl is coming to town, and I've got some ideas to get rid of your ghost friend."

"He is *not* my friend."

"What's that tone? I mean, *I know* he isn't, but you seem a little more sour about it than usual."

"I just hung up with Jack."

"Uh-oh."

"Yeah, he ended things."

"What happened? I thought things were going well."

"James Collins thinks I'm his wife and he... I don't even know how, but he attacked us last night."

"What?"

"Yeah, I even got a nosebleed from the whole thing. It took forever to stop."

"That is truly insane. Well, I've been talking to my wacky cousin. You know, the one that started studying our heritage last year?"

"You know that doesn't make her wacky, right?"

"Right, I know. She is wacky for a whole lotta other reasons, like going back to that cheating bastard that she calls bae. But you knew who I meant?"

"Yeah, Tasha, right?"

"Right. So, anyway, she finds that we have ancestors that practice some dark magic or medicine or something. They were like witch doctors, if you will, but she told me about these cleansing things you can do in the house. She gave me all the instructions. Do you still have some of his clothing?"

"Yeah, I have a few things still in the attic."

"Great, we'll need those."

"And she thinks this will work?" I was willing to try just about anything if it got rid of this spirit.

Now today, I was washing the sheets after my guests checked out and waiting for Simone to arrive. She had rented a car as I wasn't able to take time off to get her and a car service would have been more expensive.

I was making the bed in the sunrise bedroom as I was calling it when I heard the familiar footsteps.

"No, not now, James."

"Don't ignore me." He growled, but the fog didn't surround me.

I continued making the bed, but then felt a cold run up my spine. It was as if someone ran a finger along it. I shivered.

That's when music filled the room. It was a classical style that you would play when waltzing or some formal dance like that. As the music got louder, the fog came.

"Dance with me. Dance with me like we used to."

His arms felt like they were holding me, then it felt as if I was floating, though I don't think my feet left the ground. He began dancing me around. Even though this wasn't violent, it felt scary and wrong.

Where are my dogs to stop him?

Please help me. I thought. I knew trying to speak was pointless.

I don't know how long he danced with me, but it finally ended. As the fog lifted, I felt his arms let go, and I fell straight forward on to the bed.

With my face buried in the pillow I had been holding, I laid there trying to process what had happened. It was a violent encounter, but I still felt violated.

I remember Anna-Rose mentioning something in her writings about James dancing with her many nights during his happier days. She didn't like it anymore than I did now.

The familiar sound of crunching gravel on the road meant I couldn't wallow long because Simone was here, and just in time. I pushed up and ran to her.

"Sorry, sorry." I said when I reached the first floor, just as she came inside.

That's when I noticed the dogs had joined us. Of course, they come running for company. Where were they when I needed them?

Looking at Tucker covered in mud, I could take a wild guess. He had recently discovered he loved the pigs' mud hole.

"Hey, girl!" She ran to me, grabbing me up in a bear hug. "I missed this face." She squeezed my cheeks.

"I hate when you do that." I laughed. "I missed you too."

"You look flush. Are you okay?"

"Yeah, I just had a weird James incident."

"Just now?"

"Yes, that's why I wasn't out here to greet you right away."

"Whoa. Tell me about it."

I gestured for her to follow me upstairs as I told her about the music and the feeling of dancing, but still frozen in place.

"And when he left, I realized I hadn't actually moved at all, but it sure felt like it."

"Well, I have the cure right here in my hot little hands." She held up her phone. "We just have to follow the instructions my cousin gave me, and she swears he will be gone."

"But how will I know he is truly gone and not just on vacation?" I didn't think ghosts took vacations, but it was the best description I could come up with.

"We don't. Just trust me and my wacky cousin. She got this from our great-great grandmothers and great-grandmothers."

She read to me the spell and the ingredients list. It was mostly a bunch of weeds and herbs.

"And we need a bonfire, but your fire pit out back should work." Simone said as she got to the end of the instructions.

"That's all weird, but I'll try just about anything at this point. He is getting in between me and a normal life." Forget that the only eligible bachelor in my age-range now won't get near me.

"Girl, we're going to take care of this dude for you. I promise."

We got her settled in the room and then headed to my garden and yard to see if we could find the necessary. After about twenty minutes of hunting the yard, we found the last henbit needed. The dogs loved us rooting around in the yard, especially Tucker.

He tried to help by digging things up. I loved him as much as I did Misty. He was a perfect addition.

"I actually like their little purple flowers."

"We're lucky there is still some growing. It's usually a spring weed." She commented.

"I didn't know that." I looked at my friend. "How do you know that?"

"I had to research all the ingredients. It was the only one I was really worried about."

"What if we wouldn't have found it?"

"She said we could try without it, but it was more potent with it."

"So, now what? Do we cook them? Wash them?"

"Nah, just lay them to dry a bit and tonight we will burn them over the fire."

"Well, alrighty."

We laid them out on paper towels and left them on the back porch. I poured us each a glass of wine and Simone took a seat on one of my bar stools by the kitchen island.

"So, what are you making us for dinner?"

"Well, I'm trying out a new recipe for a creamy garlic chicken with wild rice pilaf, along with a salad from my garden."

"Sounds yummy! I miss your cooking so much. Potlucks just aren't the same without you."

"Cooking for guests has given me much more practice and I've gotten quite a few new go-tos."

"I bet."

We chatted as I prepped and cooked, then we took our plates out to the porch.

"Ohmygosh, Linds, this is hands down the best thing I have ever eaten." Simone moaned. "This is heaven on a plate."

"Thank you. I told you I was getting even better." I beamed.

"This is heads and tails above potluck. This is restaurant level."

"I'm going to add that to my website." I stabbed at a juicy piece of chicken.

"That's just good marketing." She laughed, then scooped up a few vegetables. "These veggies are also better than anything I've ever eaten."

"They are so much better fresh from the garden, right?"

"Absolutely!"

We finished our meal, and she offered to do the dishes.

"I'm going to let you." I sat back and watched her.

James and Anna-Rose were on my mind a lot. She was as miserable with him as am I. I still hadn't gotten to the part in her journals where he dies, so I still didn't know what happened there. I had been so busy with running my business that I hadn't been able to read them.

Last time I'd read, they were in marital bliss, but she said it wouldn't last and was waiting for his temper to flare again.

Given his unpredictable behavior, I could see why she felt that way. He would be quiet for days or a week, then temper. Then the dancing today. Why? Perhaps he thought he'd won by running Jack off.

Pfft, I thought. *Nobody won in that case.*

"Done." Simone announced. "Ready to get the real party started?"

"Yes, please."

We headed to the porch. I had brought down a shirt and pants from the attic earlier, and they were sitting near the herbs and weeds. We gathered everything and headed to the fire pit. The dogs on our heels. Tucker might have been hoping for more digging.

All the fire making supplies were in a dry box near the fire pit. I had considered doing a gas fire pit, but I loved the smell of the wood burning.

Pulling out the supplies that we needed, I began the process of starting the fire. First with tinder, then adding larger and larger logs until it was at the size I wanted. We watched it as it got stronger and brighter.

"Alright, ready?" She asked.

"Yep." I grabbed the shirt and pants. "Now what?"

"We'll say the chant as we add them to the fire, followed by the plants."

"Okay."

We started the chant, reading it directly from her phone. When we got to the end, I threw first the shirt and then the pants. They took a nanosecond to catch, but once started, they burned quickly.

"Now the weeds." She instructed.

I sprinkled them into the flames and watched them catch and smoke. We watched the embers flicking and glowing. My whole body shivered as a sudden chill ran through me in the otherwise warm air. I wrapped my arms around myself. Simone did the same.

"It got cold." She stepped closer to the fire. "That must mean it's working."

"Yeah, maybe so." I had to hope it did. I could not let this ruin my new life. "Wine?"

"Yes, please."

I ran back to the house, returning with a bottle of wine and two glasses. We sat in the chairs that surrounded the fire pit.

I had only one family use this amenity so far. They had bought marshmallows, graham crackers, and chocolate. They had invited me to join them, but I let them have their family time.

We sat sipping wine, chatting, and watching the flames burn out. As the fire turned to ash, I poked it to break it up a bit. This would allow it to die better.

I faced Simone. "I guess that's it."

"Yes, it is, and the end of your pest." She wrapped her arms around me, and we stood there for another moment, taking in the night.

I felt a peace settle within me. Done. Good riddance, James Collins.

Chapter Thirty: Lindsey (August Present Day)

I stood on the porch waving to my favorite. It was my first ever guests returning for another visit. Misty and Tucker stood next to me, waiting for the kids to get out of the car. The second they did, Misty was there with Tucker close on her heels.

"Oh, you got another dog!" Lily squealed as she dropped in front of him. He licked her and wagged himself nearly in two.

"What's his name?" Colt asked, as he joined Lily.

"Tucker. He is Misty's baby."

"Can we see the animals now?" Paige asked hopefully.

"After we get checked in." Hilary said. "Hi Lindsey, it's so good to see you again."

She came over to hug me.

"I'm so glad y'all could get back out here to visit us again."

They grabbed bags, and we went in so I could get them checked in. As they didn't need a tour, they headed straight up to get settled in the rooms.

While they did that, I went to the kitchen to make sure I had everything ready for their snack, even though the kids would likely want to skip it in favor of seeing the animals.

I went to wait on the back porch, but I didn't wait long. The trio came bursting out the door, eager to see all the animals. Parents were a second or two behind.

"So, important question for you: do you want cookies and lemonade, or visit the animals first?"

"Animals!" the siblings yelled.

"Well, if you're sure." I laughed. "But remember the rules about no sudden movements or running around them, right?"

"We remember." Paige said.

"Then let's go."

We made our way to the barnyard. The animals came running. I had a good system now for keeping the wandering animals inside the yard. I gestured for the family to follow me into the barn, then I closed the barn gate, and we entered the yard through the barn.

"Lily goat likes to escape, or at least she tries, every time that outer gate opens."

Human Lily giggled.

I gave the kids cups of pellets and they jumped right into feeding the various animals.

"Which one is Colt?" Colt asked, pointing at the donkeys.

"That one there. The gray one."

He went over to greet Donkey Colt. The donkey had quite a big personality and got bouncy and playful, kicking up and running around. Human Colt giggled and pointed. Hilary was there for all the pictures. They were perfect moments.

I leaned back on the fence as I watched the kids. Paige was laughing, interacting with her family and animals, and not sulking or pouting like last time. The other two kids had grown an inch each, but otherwise, they all looked the same as in early summer.

After a while, the animals settled down to nap. The kids got a little bored, so I suggested a snack.

"But first, let's get washed up." Zane told his kids.

They moaned a little, but marched upstairs to the bathroom. I took the snack out to the porch for them, getting it all set up. They all came back down and dug in.

The kids told me about the rest of their summer.

"And grandma and grandpa came to stay with us. We got to eat pizza and ice cream."

"Oh, and watch movies."

"You get to eat pizza, ice cream, and watch movies with us," Zane protested.

"Yeah, but grandma and grandpa let us do it without doing chores." Colt replied.

"No chores!" Lily chanted.

"Oh, you like that, huh?" Zane teased.

To allow them to enjoy family time, I excused myself. I went into the kitchen to prep for dinner. Tonight's menu would be a roast chicken, so it would take some time to cook. I remember the children loved chicken.

Once that was going and the kitchen cleaned, I went and gathered the cookie tray and lemonade glasses. The family was playing a game of horseshoes. I watched for only a second, not wanting to stare.

Hours later, chores done, dinner done, and family settled in upstairs, I stood in the quiet living room listening. Thankfully, I didn't hear anything unusual from the ghost. He had been quiet the past week since Simone had left. I hoped that was the end of things.

I'm sure I would be on edge, always wondering if and when he would pop up again. But I had to have faith that Simone's spell had taken care of him.

The next morning, I was up bright and early to get breakfast going for the family. Today was French toast, sausage links, and fruit. I had everything set up on my side table in the dining room when they came downstairs.

"Yum. Everything smells as good as always." Hilary said, as she started helping Lily and Colt get breakfast. Zane headed straight for coffee, and Paige just wanted to know when they could help with the animals.

"After breakfast."

I went back into the kitchen while they ate. I was nearly done cleaning when I heard them finishing up.

"Anyone need anything else?" I asked.

"So, full." Colt said.

"It was lovely. Thank you." Hilary added.

"Then are we ready to feed the animals?"

"Yay!" the children cheered.

"Oh, no, I forgot. I didn't put my shoes on." Lily said, "I'll be right back."

Everyone laughed. I started clearing the breakfast dishes. Paige jumped up to help me.

"Aw, aren't you sweet? You know I don't require chores here."

"I know, but I don't mind." She grinned as she grabbed plates and cups.

We carried it into the kitchen, and I began rinsing them. She went back to grab more. That's when we heard it. A thud followed by a blood-curdling scream from Lily. Hilary called out and two sets of footsteps could be heard running up the stairs. I quickly followed them.

When I made it upstairs, I found a hysterical Lily being comforted by her mother. Her face was red, tears streaming down it, but I couldn't understand what she was saying.

"Slow down, baby. What happened?" Hilary whispered calmly.

"I was getting my shoes, but I couldn't find the left one." She said through sobs and hiccups. "Then, suddenly, I couldn't move and I couldn't see. It was like I was in a fog or cloud or something."

My stomach twisted as I realized what had happened. I gasped. All eyes turned to me.

"Is she okay? Are you okay?" I said.

"I think she is, but what happened next?" Hilary said, turning back to the still violently crying child.

"A voice... a man's voice was screaming about how children are selfish and something about not wanting children." She collapsed into her mother with full on wailing cries.

Hilary rubbed her back but looked over at me. Her death stare sent chills through me. Did she know I knew about him? Was she blaming me?

"What was that?" She asked. "Is this something you did? Some sick joke?"

"No, how would I...? Why would I do that?"

"It was a ghost." Lily cried.

"Oh, baby, there are no ghosts." Hilary said, but then looked at her husband. "Are there?"

"Well, I had heard something about this place being haunted." He said. "But I had heard nothing serious, just a rumor."

They all looked at me again. The looks were accusing, questioning, hate filled. I hesitated only a moment, but I knew I'd need to come clean, no matter how crazy it made me sound.

"I... yes, there is a ghost, but he has never attacked a guest before. He only messes with me."

"Clearly, he does not." She snapped, as she continued to comfort her child. "Zane, start packing our things. We are *not* staying here a minute longer."

I wanted to argue. I wanted to fight, but I knew there was no point. James had gone after their child. That was unforgivable.

Colt and Paige started crying along with Lily, but nobody spoke again to me.

"I will refund your stay, plus a night's worth." I mumbled as I left the room.

I would not fall apart in front of them. At the front desk, I began compensating them, plus I added a little more for the inconvenient situation. I knew I couldn't recover from this. It was all over. My dream of running this beautiful bed-and-breakfast was done.

James had made sure of that. He got his revenge on Anna-Rose.

I could almost hear his evil laugh echoing in the hallway.

"You are mine, and mine alone." His voice whispered.

Minutes later, the family came down, the children still crying. The parents with red faces and tension radiating off of them.

"I'm very sorry." I offered.

"We will never come back here, and we will be leaving a review about this," Hilary snarled.

She slammed the door after her. The entire house seemed to rattle for seconds after. I stood at the window watching them load up; the parents yelling at each other and the stubborn children who did not want to leave, despite the ghost.

Only Lily was silent. Her eyes were wide and red, but her breathing seemed normal now.

She looked at the house. When she saw me, she smiled weakly and lifted her hand to wave, but Hilary caught the movement and snapped for her to get in the car. Hilary then turned to shoot me a look.

I backed up into the shadows, but where I could still watch them leave. It was a hopeless feeling as the car turned left toward the freeway.

"James Collins, I am done with you."

Chapter Thirty-One: Anna-Rose (1884)

It was August. Hot and humid during the day, hot and humid at night. We left the windows open to catch any bit of air we could, but we had to be cautious of raccoons, rats, or opossums coming in them.

"We should get a dog or two." I suggested to James. "They will keep the pests away."

"Dogs are just as selfish as children. Always looking for a handout or attention. No."

His foot was down on that one. The other issue with having the windows open was you could hear every single sound coming from outside. At least when they were closed, there was a slight buffer and I could forget that there were bears, wolves, and other predators out there.

It became harder to ignore when they took out our livestock. We lost about a dozen over the course of a month. It seemed like the smart thing to do was get a couple of dogs and maybe a few donkeys. Donkeys were extremely territorial and would defend their herd against anything they saw as a threat.

He didn't like either idea. Instead, he paid his men extra to take turns standing watch each night over the herd. It seemed to work for a few weeks, until one night, a pack of wolves mauled one of his men. He died alone in the field. Since they kept the cattle were kept so far from the house, we hadn't heard a thing.

James and his other men found him the next morning, along with a calf.

But instead of just getting a few dogs, James had his men build a new barn with a large corral attached. The barn was just one large room, no stalls.

His idea was to stuff his cattle in there each night, or at least most of them. He left his bull and the older cows outside the barn, but still within the new yard.

"It will make it easier to watch over them this way."

It didn't make sense to me, but what did I know?

"If something tries to attack, we will be close by and can assist."

I simply nodded as he explained. He would not listen to my suggestions, so I didn't waste my words.

It was during this time that I realized I was expecting again. I was heart broke and thrilled at the same time. James would likely kill it, so I didn't dare get too attached, but I hoped for the best. After all, he had wanted to try.

I kept it to myself for as long as I could; he was dealing with enough. Since I never had sickness, he wouldn't know until my stomach showed.

One night, he noticed. It was his turn to stand watch, so he had gone into nap before his shift. He wanted me to wake him after a few hours.

"Are you sure, James? You get so angry when I wake you." I tried to laugh at the end, but it was the truth.

"It is important, Anna-Rose. We could lose everything if they continue to kill our livestock." He snarled, but then his tone softened. "I'm sorry. I shouldn't take my anger and frustrations out on you. I am trying."

"I will wake you."

He nodded and went to the bedroom. I watched the clock waiting for the right time. As the sunset, his men drove the cows into the barn and yard for us. They tipped their hats as they left. I grabbed the shotgun and unofficially stood watch over them until I could no longer see into the darkness.

It was time to wake James.

Grabbing the oil lamp, I set the gun down as I turned the light up, then taking a deep breath, I entered the room, but I ensured I stood across from him. I did not want to get within striking distance.

"James, dear, it's time for your watch." I whispered.

"Um, what?" His voice growled.

"You asked me to wake you."

"I know what I asked." He snarled. He was a grump to wake.

"Okay." I backed out of the room.

I could hear the bed creak and groan as he stood, then he stomped a few times before marching out. I was standing frozen in the hallway. He touched me.

"Are you...? Anna-Rose, what is going on with your stomach?"

"I... you wanted us to try to, and now we are expecting." I tried to sound cheerful, but I was petrified.

"I didn't want this. You tricked me." His hand came fast and hard across my face.

I backed down the hallway toward the kitchen. He followed; his eyes were red from lack of sleep but also anger.

"James, please, don't murder another child."

"Murder? Ha, I made that *thing*, so I have the final say on what happens to it." His tone was menacing as he snarled the hate filled words at me.

I tried to keep a distance from him, but he charged on me so quickly. I fell back and hit my head on the door. If I could get outside, put some distance between us, maybe I could be safe. But he was on me, screaming, punching, slapping me.

Stars were circling my head. The only thing I could see were his eyes. His blood-shot eyes full of rage and hate.

"Why do you hate me so?" I choked out.

That stopped him for long enough that I could catch my breath, even slightly.

"Hate you? No, Anna-Rose, I love you. I love you so much that it hurts. It hurts that you want some... *thing* to come between us. A selfish thing." He pushed away from me. He ran a hand down his face as I lay on the floor.

That's when I saw it. The rifle was just within my reach. If I could get it and then get outside, perhaps I had a chance still. I waited only a heartbeat as I tried to get my breathing a bit more even.

He turned toward the sink and began washing his face. That was my chance. I lunged forward, grabbing it and then bolted outside.

"Damn it, Anna-Rose!" His footsteps came after me, but I was running. I ran to the outhouse, thinking to get on the other side of it and hide. It was, in my opinion, the darkest part of the yard.

I didn't quite make it before he was on me again, trying to wrestle the gun from my hands.

"James, stop. Please, please let me keep this child." I cried.

"Give me the gun before you hurt yourself."

We struggled and rolled around on the ground, but I was not letting go. This was my only hope. He backhanded me once, twice, but on the third time he went to rear-back, I managed to wiggle out from under him. I aimed the gun at him.

"Stop right there, James Collins, or I will shoot you." My voice came out braver and harsher than I knew I could speak.

"No, you won't. You are just a woman. A weak, weak woman." He stood and took a few steps toward me, but I squeezed the hammer.

I heard it hit, and he went down hard. He didn't even cry out until he had hit the ground. The pain of the recoil shot through me, but the adrenaline kept me going.

The first shot went through his stomach, just inches from his heart. I wanted him to suffer, so I stepped forward, putting a second in his thigh. It should be just enough for him to bleed out, but perhaps make it look as if it was an accident.

"I told you to stop." I snarled.

His breathing was garbled and weak. "Anna-Rose… no…"

That was all I heard. His breathing seemed to have slowed or maybe stopped. I couldn't tell and didn't want to get close enough to find out.

I backed away from him. Now what do I do? I killed him, but it needed to look like I hadn't. That's when I got an idea.

I went to the cow barn. Taking a nearby rake, I scratched and clawed at the door until it broke open.

"Did that look like a wolf did it?" I shrugged.

Next, I got a bucket and started banging it as loud and hard as I could. Cows reared and stomped, letting out a horrible cry. They began running in all directions except, luckily for me, they didn't come near the sound. I tried to direct them in James' direction.

That would cover up what happened and if someone questioned me, I would cry and admit that I had shot him, but it was because I missed a wolf.

"Yes, that should work."

In the faint light from the moon and house, I could see that they had run over him. If he had survived the shots, that would finish him.

Next, I threw the rake and bucket into my garden area and then ran into the house, out of the way of any other stray cows. I checked my reflection in the mirror. It was believable that something had happened here.

I grabbed the lantern this time, turning off the oil lamp. The lantern was better for what I was going to do next.

I ran down the long driveway and turned right toward town.

"Help! Help me." I yelled when I got to the nearest house.

I was crying and in pain. Only the tears were fake, partially fake. I cried with relief to be done with him. But the pain was real, and I knew what it would likely mean. This time I would be okay with it. Having him out of my life was worth the cost.

I could hear voices, and lights flickered in the windows.

"Help... my husband..." I gasped and then collapsed from the pain. It was over. I was finally free.

Chapter Thirty-Two: Lindsey (August Present Day)

After the Brookwoods left, I let myself fall apart. I melted to the floor in a heap of tears and despair. He had ruined my entire life. My new life, the one I had built for myself.

He scared my favorite guests and my first date in years.

"Why? Why me?" I cried to the ceiling.

"Because you killed me." His voice seemed to come from right above me.

"I am not your wife. I'm not Anna-Rose. I don't know you." I screamed out. "You died more than a hundred years ago."

"But you are the one who did it. I will never forget. You shot me."

I cursed and screamed, pounding my fists on the ground. I knew it was a full-on toddler tantrum, but in this moment, I simply did not care. Thankfully, the dogs had gone outside after the family left. They weren't here to witness my terror.

That's when I had an idea. As I stood up, I wiped roughly at my eyes, wiping at the angry tears. I rummaged in the drawer in the reception counter until I found my USB drive. I plugged it into my computer and then started the systems back-up program.

While that updated, I went to my room; I threw all my important papers into a bag. Then I grabbed a small duffel, filling it full of things I would need for a few nights away. I moved room to room, gathering all the things I deemed irreplaceable.

I threw everything into my truck, but then thought it would be better to hide them on the far side of the barn. The barn's office was in the back, away from the house, so that should do it.

This included Anna-Rose's journals and the ceramic figurine that I had found in the attic. I couldn't save all the trunks; it would look too suspicious. What I was planning was risky enough.

"I have to pack lightly, but smart."

I slide the dog door insert into place. That way, the dogs couldn't come back inside.

Next, I took a few of the face plates off the wall outlets. I didn't know a lot about electrical work, but I knew enough about how to make it spark and burn. During a construction job with my dad, I learned that the hard way.

I repeated those fatal steps now. As it smoldered, I happily inhaled the burning smell. I put the wall plates back. I repeated that step over and over again until I was satisfied. Next, I moved to the kitchen; I turned the gas on just enough to leak. I wanted it slow enough that I could get out and away before it went boom.

I took a last look around my beautiful home and business. My memories began of all the shared laughs among my guests and friends. I could smell the wonderful, delicious meals I had cooked in this kitchen.

I stood in my beautiful kitchen at the farmhouse sink pointed at the morning sunrise and the barnyard, where I often watched my animals jumping and playing.

"I'm going to miss this house so very much."

A few tears slide down my face, but I could smell the gas collecting in the room and knew I had to get out now. It was going to blow soon, and I needed to be far away when it did.

I went out the back door and headed straight to the truck. I had parked it far enough away and hoped to heck that the barnyard was far enough back that if what I expected to happen did, in fact, happen, it would be safe.

Just in case, I moved all the animals into the barn and to the farthest stalls away from the house. Then I parked the trailer in front of the outer wall.

"I hope this works."

I called the dogs and got them loaded into the truck. I slowly drove away. As I often did, I looked in the rearview mirror to take in my house. That is when I noticed smoke and the first flicks of flames starting.

I took a right and headed to town. My first stop would be the library to drop off these journals to Brenda, and I would give her the ceramic figurine as well.

I slide the truck into a spot in front of the library. The dogs and I hopped out, I grabbed the box with Anna-Rose's things, and then pushed the library door open. The familiar chime above the door sounded, signaling someone had arrived.

"Well, hey, there Lindsey. I wasn't expecting you today." She leaned over to pet the dogs.

They were welcome nearly everywhere in town, which I loved. I didn't know yet what I was going to do. Build again in a new spot on the land or move on. Can't think about that now. I put on a neutral face.

"Yeah, I am done with Anna-Rose's journals and thought I should return them."

"Oh, well, that's sweet. I didn't expect them back, but happy that you read them. Learn anything?"

I thought about all I had learned about Anna-Rose. She was a smart, strong woman. She had put up with a lot of abuse, but when the time came, she put her foot down, in a big way. Even if I wasn't her reincarnated, I liked to think I was a lot like her.

"Yes, I did. She was an interesting person. I wish I would have known her."

She smiled and took the box from me.

"Oh, and I threw in an extra surprise. A figurine I'd found in the attic. Something about it spoke to me. I think she would have wanted it with her other things." Something inside me said yes.

Suddenly, someone burst into the library. It was Emily, the mayor.

"Lindsey, oh, good you're here." She was out of breath. "I saw your truck here." She hooked her thumb over her shoulder.

"Is something wrong?" I faked surprise.

"Your house is on fire."

"Oh, no!" I looked at Brenda.

"Go. Of course, go."

I got the dogs loaded into the truck and thanked Emily as I faked rushing away. Once out of view, I took my time.

There was nothing to rush to. I had already seen my handy work in the rearview mirror. It wasn't like I was going to save it, and didn't want to even if I could.

The police and several fire trucks blocked most of my driveway, so I couldn't get too close to the house. I cracked the windows for the dogs and told them to stay.

I put on my best panicked face as I looked around.

"Oh, my gosh. My house!" I cried, dropping to my knees.

An officer came forward. "This is your place?"

"Yes, what... what happened?"

She filled me in on what she knew.

"What about my animals?" I tried to go toward the barn. She stopped me.

"Were they in the house?"

"No, the barn. Is the barn okay?"

"A little damage, but it is mostly cosmetic to the barn. The blast wasn't big enough to take that out. We have the gas line turned off now."

"Oh, thank goodness. They should be okay, then."

"Yes." She began asking me questions, and I answered them all. "Do you have somewhere to stay? Do you need anything?"

"I guess I can call the motel. I always keep extra clothes in the barn for emergencies." That sounded plausible, right?

"Okay." She laid a hand on my shoulder and then turned back to the scene.

I stood there watching it burn. That's when I heard it. The dying sound on the wind.

"Why, Anna-Rose, why?"

"You know why." I whispered.

"But I love you."

"Go to hell, James Collins." Then I turned my back, headed to my truck, and made my way back to town. It was over.

Chapter Thirty-Three: Anna-Rose (1945)

I was laying in my bed, staring out at the barn. It was now empty, not having animals housed in it for at least ten years. Sometimes I missed them so much. They had been my family when I had no one else.

After James died, I sold off all the cattle. I kept my two milk cows, even after they dried up. They were dear to me. I simply got a new milk cow and over time, milk came from the milk man instead of the cow.

Same with chickens, pigs, and all the other things I used to get food from. As things advanced, I bought from the General Store or neighbors instead of doing it myself. I needed little being only one person.

Though I continued my gardening until I couldn't physically do it any longer. It had given me wonderful crops all those years, but more than that, it was something I enjoyed doing. It reminded me of simpler times, sitting in the garden, listening to the wind and birds.

I have lived a beautiful life these past sixty-one years. Though I never remarried or had children, it was still a happy life. Full of friends, the church and I'd given to the town my time and love. I got to enjoy this wonderful land on my terms without fear.

Though James's soul seemed to live on in the house, I had learned to control him. I always kept dogs and people around. He didn't like it, but he was quieter in those busy times.

I could feel him here often, but he couldn't hurt or control me any longer. I was free to eat when and what I wanted, wear what I wanted.

After my nightmare of a marriage, I also made the choice not to marry again. I didn't even date. I simply explained it off, as I was still in love with my deceased husband. It wasn't a complete lie that I didn't want to marry again because of him, but it was only because he had soured me on men.

I no longer had a dog or any pets, but I had people around me, especially since having a stroke last year. I required around-the-clock help.

During the day and overnight, it would be a lady or two from the church. They would help while the children were in school.

After school and during the summer months, I would have teen girls help me. They were so sweet, always wanting to help me with anything and everything they could. Such caring young people.

Even before my stroke, I had hired the girls. It was their job to help around the house with chores. Sometimes during the summer months, they would live here.

Before my stroke, these girls would help me around the farm. It would prepare them for their future lives here in Wisteria as so many families ran farms.

Today, I had Edie here. She was a quiet girl, but strong and willing to help with all my chores that I couldn't do for myself any longer.

"Here you are, Ms. Anna-Rose," Edie said, as she came into my room. She had a bowl of soup with crackers and a glass of water. "Do you need help to eat?"

"Thank you, dear. I can manage." I tried to sit up but couldn't. "Can you help me sit up?"

"Of course."

She got me up and seated better, then draped the napkin under my chin.

"I'll be close by if you need me." She smiled and left the room.

I took the spoon and scooped up a bit of the broth. Despite the tremors, I got it into my mouth. It took me longer to eat, but I didn't call for Edie. I sipped my water as I looked outside.

A mockingbird was sitting on the fence not far away. I watched him. I loved all the birds that visited outside my window.

The crows had always been my favorite, though. They were mighty and smart, cunning, and majestic. People didn't always like them, thinking they were bad luck or ugly. I loved them.

"All finished?" Edie said, coming in. "Let me take that from you."

She took the tray of dishes to the kitchen, but returned quickly.

"Would you like to sit outside for a bit?"

"No, thank you. I think I will just stay here for now."

"No problem. Can I get you anything? A book, the newspaper?"

"Can you throw some scraps for the birds? Throw them outside the window so I may see them."

"Of course. I will do it right now."

Moments later, I saw the girl with the kitchen bucket we used to hold scraps. She was throwing them just as I'd directed. She looked my way once. I smiled.

I could feel myself growing weaker and knew my time here was nearing the end. The when part was a mystery, but I hoped it would be in my sleep while I dreamed of something peaceful and free.

If I got a second chance at life, I wouldn't let a man control me. I would love to have a big family with lots of love. But the most important thing was that I lived here in Wisteria on this land. It was my home.

I don't even know if I believe in reincarnation, but I liked the idea of getting a second chance at life. A chance to do the things that I didn't get to during this one.

I drifted off to sleep, watching the birds and reflecting. I woke hours later to a dark, quiet house. Edie would have gone home. I wonder who was here to help me now.

I pushed myself up carefully. It was difficult, and I got winded, but I managed to swing my legs over the side of the bed. Nearby was my cane, so I used it to lean on as I made my way to the bathroom. I loved having indoor plumbing. I hadn't used an outhouse in so many years, I barely remembered it.

I laughed a little at the thought. *That's where he died.*

After I'd relieved myself, I continued down the hallway and into the living room. On the couch was Diana. She was the daughter of the current pastor. She was sound asleep, so I let her be and continued to the kitchen.

I wanted water.

I reached the kitchen, out of breath and mildly dizzy. As I so rarely got out of bed by myself, it took a lot of physical effort these days. Things got blurry when I reached for a glass. I knew what was coming.

I hit the floor. In the surrounding fog, I heard his laugh. I knew it was him. He was here.

"See you in hell, James Collins."

The End

Before you go: If you loved The Haunting of Anna-Rose. You may be interested in my other paranormal books. By visiting my website and signing up for my newsletter, you will receive a copy of Unsolved Murder, the prequel to my Medium with a Heart, Paranormal cozy mystery series.

Also below, you can find my grandmother's chocolate cake recipe. Let's just pretend it's Anna-Rose's.

www.ejwheltonwrites.com

Growing up, we had Sunday dinner most weeks, and we celebrated all the holidays together. My paternal grandmother used to make this chocolate cake for many of those. When I thought of Anna-Rose sharing her chocolate cake recipe with the museum, this is what I pictured.

Now I'm not saying my grandmother's recipe was something she made up. I'm sure she got it from a newspaper or magazine article, but it is something I associate with her. Enjoy!

Chocolate Moist and Easy Cake:

2 cups flour
1 cup sugar
1 ½ tsp baking soda
1 ½ tsp baking powder
4 tbsp cocoa
1 cup water
1 cup salad dressing
2 tsp vanilla

Mix all ingredients together. Bake in 13x9 inch pan for 35 minutes at 350 degrees. Cool and ice in pan.

Icing:

1 cup sugar
¼ cup cocoa
¼ cup milk
¼ cup margarine
1 tsp vanilla

Boil together for 3 minutes. Pour over cake.

Made in the USA
Monee, IL
13 June 2023

35692363R00132